On the Edge

The Apache drew a long knife from his belt, then ran his mount hell-bent into Slocum's mare.

The collision threw Slocum and his horse into the sand. Somewhere during the impact he'd lost his Colt. The mare's frantic effort to get herself up gave Slocum enough time to look for his gun. No pistol in sight.

The Apache veered from his course to get at Slocum. With enraged, violent screams, he charged across the last, short space to drive his knife into his enemy's heart. The day had come. Slocum had nothing but his bare hands, and he prepared for the last fight of his life . . .

DON'T MISS THESE
ALL-ACTION WESTERN SERIES
FROM THE BERKLEY PUBLISHING GROUP

JAKE LOGAN

SLOCUM AND THE LONG RIDE

J

JOVE BOOKS, NEW YORK

THE BERKLEY PUBLISHING GROUP
Published by the Penguin Group
Penguin Group (USA) LLC
375 Hudson Street, New York, New York 10014

USA • Canada • UK • Ireland • Australia • New Zealand • India • South Africa • China

penguin.com

A Penguin Random House Company

SLOCUM AND THE LONG RIDE

A Jove Book / published by arrangement with the author

For information, address: The Berkley Publishing Group,
a division of Penguin Group (USA) LLC,
375 Hudson Street, New York, New York 10014.

ISBN: 978-0-515-15385-9

PUBLISHING HISTORY
Jove mass-market edition / November 2013

PRINTED IN THE UNITED STATES OF AMERICA

10 9 8 7 6 5 4 3 2 1

Cover illustration by Sergio Giovine.

This is a work of fiction. Names, characters, places, and incidents either are the product
of the author's imagination or are used fictitiously, and any resemblance to actual persons,
living or dead, business establishments, events, or locales is entirely coincidental.

1

There were spirals of black smoke against the azure sky all around him. Ranch headquarters were being burned down by Apache war parties up and down the Sulphur Springs Valley. He pushed his lathered horse south for the Pitch Fork Ranch. A man he knew well, Oran Oglethorpe, had the largest ranch crew in that country, and if anyone could hold off the damn Chiricahua Apaches, he and his Texans could at their place, and by damn Slocum was going to try to get there before the Apaches caught him out in the open.

He rode past the one-room Simon Flat Schoolhouse and noticed that the front door was wide open. Was someone in there? *Oh hell.* He reined the gelding up, then spun him around him on his heels and headed him toward the open door, pounding him with his spurs to hurry. In a flying dismount he hit the ground on his boot heels, and rowels clanging, six-gun in his fist, he threw back the door. Ready for anything—

A young woman, seated at a desk on the foot-higher

stage, who at the sight of him and his drawn gun screamed, "Who are you?"

"No, lady, what in the hell are you doing out here? This whole damn country is alive with bloodthirsty savages. Come on. We've only got a few minutes to get the hell out of here."

She had long brown hair. He guessed her to be eighteen. Her breasts molded the white blouse she wore, and the hem of her long brown skirt rested on her buttoned shoe tops. Standing at her desk, she looked to be indignant about his orders.

"Come on. Those Apaches are damn sure coming." He was growing impatient with her frowning and the hesitation aimed at him.

"I'm getting ready for my classes next week. Who are you?"

He caught her by the arm and she slapped him. Not letting go, he holstered his gun and dragged her to the doorway. Then he looked both ways before hauling her with him out on the porch. Nothing was in sight, so he headed her for his hard-breathing, lathered horse and caught the reins.

"Now I'll get in the saddle and then put you up behind me."

"I can't straddle that horse in this skirt."

"Take it off then."

"No. It would be too indecent to do that."

His firm grip on her arm drew her face close to his. "What's worse, being embarrassed or dead?"

"All right. I'll take it off."

He hoisted himself into the saddle. She tossed him the skirt and then took his stirrup to mount. He pulled her up in place. "Hang on, girl. We've got to ride like hell out of here."

Looking down to check on her position, he saw the frilly

white lace slip's hem and a nice bare leg beside his chap-covered one. No time for that, he simply hoped the bay horse had ten more miles of go left in him to carry the two of them to the Pitch Fork. They were off in a lurch, but she'd ridden before from behind someone else and knew to wrap her arms around his waist. Her firm breasts molded two spots in his back.

"Who are you?" she asked behind his ear as the pony caught his gait again.

"Folks call me Slocum."

"Where do you live?"

"Where I sleep."

"You have no home."

"Nope—no home, no woman—nothing but what you can see on this worn-out horse."

"You're a drifter?"

"You might say that. I've spent lots of my time figuring out how to stay alive in this world."

"Are you wanted?"

"Good question." He spurred the horse to get more out of him as they thundered though a grove of dusty junipers that lined the road. A great place, he considered, to get jumped by a war party who were burning up everything in sight.

"Where is the army?" she asked. "Aren't they supposed to protect these people?"

"There's only so many soldiers and thousands of acres of land in this territory and the one next door, New Mexico. They can't cover it all, and when the Apaches know they're in another area, they can raid unscathed in the last one the army left."

The horse's breath was rasping in his throat and he'd slowed some. Slocum wished they could find some other horses, loose ones or run-off ones—to replace him, but he hadn't seen any sign of those in the past two hours since he turned down the Sulphur Springs Valley and discovered the outbreak that must be unfolding.

She twisted behind him to look around. "Are those streaks in the sky I can see all burned down ranches?"

"Some may only be haystacks, but yes, they attack and burn you out if you can be burned."

"How many people have they killed so far?"

He thought about the little girl he'd seen lying in the dust in her blue dress, her blue eyes like the eyes of a china doll head staring into the hard midday sun. A few feet from her, her mother's naked body was sprawled on its back—she'd been ravaged, raped, and then butchered. Even considering it again, he had a hard time keeping the sourness behind his tongue down and not throwing up. The woman's white flesh glowed in the high summer sun, and the blood wasn't even dry from her scarlet knife wounds.

Back to reality, he reined the bay hard to the right with "Hang on, sister" for her. Next they busted into the juniper boughs and he reined up the horse. "Get down and hold him."

He drew the rifle out of the scabbard and checked the cylinder. It was loaded.

"Trouble?"

"There's some riders coming out of the west. I hope they're so hell-bent on something they didn't see us."

"Could they be our—" But the *ki-yack*ing coyote-like war cries carried to them, and her complexion whitened. "They're Apaches all right."

He nodded with the Winchester in his sweaty hands. He dried his right hand on his leather chaps and then went back to holding the wooden stock and trigger.

"How many?" she whispered.

"A handful. Be still. If they don't hear this horse heaving, we may avoid them."

"Sorry I doubted you. They really are on the warpath," she whispered. Her shoulders trembled under the blouse. The war party had drawn up at the road, judging from the sounds of their milling horses hidden by the thick junipers.

"Just so they don't see our tracks," Slocum said, with his heart pounding in his rib cage. His ear strained for any give-away of the Apaches' intentions in the guttural words of them arguing over something that meant nothing to him. He could hear the excitement in their untranslated words, and their horses plunged around, their nostrils no doubt filled with gun smoke, blood, and sweat. The excitement of killing and raping must feed those bucks. He'd been in their villages many times. They lounged around like they had nothing to do. Let the squaws do all the work, then they'd ride up a canyon and slay a deer, ride back to camp and simply tell a squaw where to go get it. She'd have to skin and dress it—dry the meat into jerky and tan the hide for clothing. While he sat around in camp having had day-dreams of being on the warpath.

Then the close-by Apaches left screaming, going east—didn't even use the road. Instead they rode off into the can-yons of the towering Chiricahua range of mountains on their left. The rifle back in its place, Slocum gathered her skirt from the saddle seat where he'd laid it and wadded it into his saddlebags. With a sigh of relief he remounted the horse. "That was a good thing—they've rode off."

Numb-like, she agreed and took his arm.

Bent over to help her, he hoisted her up behind him. "We're still a long ways from the Pitch Fork."

"How many are out there? Indians I mean."

He was too busy to answer her. He searched around before riding out into the open-grass and yucca-clad range-land. The two of them were off again in a rocking lope and headed south as hard as he felt he could make the horse run into the hot afternoon wind.

"Keep ahold of me. I have no idea how many there are, maybe two dozen. Tomorrow there could be as few as ten, or more than thirty. Apaches are strange—if they wake up after a bad dream, they won't ride off into warfare. This might be the day they get killed otherwise."

"Can they tell fortunes?" He felt her push herself up closer to the high back cantle on his saddle, and she held him looser, like she was more at ease with the pony's stride. They went down into a low spot where a clear small creek ran across the road.

He shook his head at her question. "If they could, they'd never get shot."

"Where did that water come from?" she asked, slipping down to the ground when he stopped. Ever alert he listened to some ravens in the distance and distinguished them from the Indians' yacking.

"A big spring. Go upstream, get a drink, and fill my canteen. I'm going to walk this hot horse and water him some. Be easy to colic him on water here and him get stiff from not moving."

"He's sure tired his heart out packing us. Good care might save him."

Slocum nodded, pulled the horse's head up dripping from the water source, and walked away with him. She had gone a ways out of sight. He turned his back to the direction she went and stopped to drain his own bladder in the road dust. Finished, he buttoned up his fly and heard her coming back.

"Something is dead up there. Maybe you should check and see what it is. I can lead the horse. It may be an animal, but it doesn't smell like one." She put the refilled canteen's strap over the saddle horn.

He gave her the reins as she flattened out her slip against

the wind's efforts to expose her bare legs. She apologized, "I know we are in very desperate straits here, but I am still a woman with concerns about acting like I was taught."

"No problem." He hurried up the cow path beside the small stream, and he could soon smell whatever was dead. First, he saw the gray underwear shirt pincushioned with turkey feather–fletched arrows in its back. The man had been dead for some time, and the smell of his decay about took Slocum's breath away. They'd taken his sidearm and left the empty holster. No pants, no boots—they'd removed them but had missed a rawhide cord around his neck. May have been superstitious about it as some religious thing he had. Slocum cut the cord in two with his jackknife and retrieved the heavy item attached to it.

The man was probably in his thirties, with reddish brown hair. In Slocum's hand was a heavy pouch his attackers had missed. He opened it and saw the gold nuggets. Nothing else. In disgust over the strong stench, he shook his head and escaped the brush backward to stand up and suck in some better air. He cleared his throat a few times and spat aside.

"He was a dead prospector."

"Find any ID?" she asked.

"No. But he had some gold."

"Prospector you say?"

"I think so." He put the deerskin pouch in the saddlebags on the other side of the horse. "No time to bury him. I'm surprised the vultures hadn't found him already. They must have enough humans to eat—hell, sharp as their noses are they could have smelled him halfway to Mexico City."

She never answered him. Obviously close to being real shaken over their hard situation.

"You're ready?"

Concerned-acting, she looked back that direction, and

the wind lifted the long hair into her face. She put it back in place with her fingers and shook her head. "Will they ever know who he was or what he was doing out here?"

"I doubt it. Not with no identification on him. They took his pants. Not much way to find out."

He stepped in the saddle and pulled her up behind him. "Let's ride. Heah yah, horse!"

They were off again. The horse was in a short lope. And Slocum knew in another hour he'd be nose-down dead in the road from sheer exhaustion.

"There's some horses." She pointed past him. A gray mare and another brown horse—he'd seen them come out of the draw. Their manes windswept, they eyed him suspiciously, like most horses turned out on the range did after a few months' liberty. They got skittish about folks.

He shook loose his lariat.

"You want me off?" She acted prepared to slip off his butt.

"Maybe best."

She did so, and he kicked the bay after them as they turned to run away. Whipping him with the lariat to go faster and driving after the mare, he figured the horse with her would come back to the mare if he caught her—he'd no doubt been running with her for some time.

He threw the rope, concerned about the wind gusting, but he caught her in his loop, jerked his slack, and dallied the rope on the horn. Now, if she wasn't too wild to ride, they might make the Pitch Fork before dark.

The whole time he talked to the mare, crowding in closer and taking up slack on the rope around her neck. His greatest concern was that he hoped she'd been ridden at some time. Most ranches ignored mares as saddle animals, and they were simply broodmare stock. Slocum dismounted his weary side-heaving horse, and the schoolteacher came to hold his reins for him.

"It's a pretty gray, isn't she?"

"She doesn't have many scars on her withers. I'm concerned she may not have been ridden much. We'll see."

His companion held the mare, while he unsaddled the dripping, lathered bay. Then easy-like he carried his tack around to transfer it to the gray. He caught a look in her eye of anarchy. Then the mare danced a little away from him when the wet blankets settled on her back. All the time in a soft low voice he spoke to try to settle her distrust and distract her. The saddle on her back, she flew backward, hit the end of the rope with him while he also held the saddle in place. When the gray reached the end of that rope but the saddle was still on her, she stood and trembled as he cinched it up.

The bit in her mouth took some doing. But he fought her down.

He noticed the schoolteacher had been holding the weary bay with the lariat and how she'd talked to the now curious loose brown horse. "I think I can catch him," she said.

"Bay won't go nowhere, catch her buddy," he said. Considering talents as she tried to coax the gelding, he decided his rig was secure on the mare's back, and he swung up in the saddle. She did buck around in a small circle, but it was only halfhearted. He gouged her with his spurs and she leaped forward—no buck for fifty feet when he set her down and she slid to a halt. Whirled around, she raced back, and his partner was holding the brown one on a lariat. Then she jumped up to lay over the horse's back, and he moved around for her. "He's broke. I'll ride him."

"I can get you a blanket to sit on." He felt concerned letting her riding bareback.

"No time for that." She sat herself up on the horse's back,

using the lariat on his head for a bridle. "My name is Saundra by the way. Saundra Brown."

"Nice to met you, Miss Brown."

"*Mrs.* Brown, I am a widow. My husband was shot and
killed by bank robbers in a small town where we lived in
Kansas. I prefer being called Sandy. I am here to help over-
come my own losses and make myself useful to society. I
thought teaching might be a good way help my fellow
Americans."

"Fine kettle of fish you got yourself in here. Let's ride."

"What about your other horse?"

"He'll be fine. We need to hurry."

They raced off. He could see that her silk slip drawn up
was showing lots of her snow-white leg. She was no stranger
to horseback riding or to doing it bareback. The fresh horses
sent them off racing hard again. Riding side by side, he
smiled at her. "You are a great horsewoman."

"I have been a tomboy all my life. I need something to
tie my hair back and keep it out of my face." He stripped the
blue-and-white silk kerchief from around his neck. "This
will do it. We can stop on that next ridge and you can tie
it up."

"Good," she shouted back. With her knees, she turned
the brown horse out in the grass and missed the near dry
mud-hole mess that once had stuck a rig in the middle of
the road.

He took the other side and they rejoined. Skidding to a
stop on the high point, he looked over the country that
spread down the valley while she bound up her hair to stay
back while they rode. He wished for a sombrero for her.
She'd be sunburnt by the time they reached the Pitch Fork.

"Wear my hat," he said, holding it out to her.

"What will you do about the sun?"

"I can find something later. Let's ride," he said when she

got his weather-beaten Stetson on her head. To keep it on she drew up the strings that he hardly used, and they were off again.

The day was waning in the west when he at last saw the red tile roofs of the Pitch Fork headquarters. Men with rifles were running around getting ready to fight the intruders. A lookout on one of the roofs shouted, "Let them in."

The two shared a confident nod when they rode under the gate crossbar with the ranch name on it. Slocum looked back, but there was no pursuit. Good.

2

The smiling ranch owner came out of the house putting on his white hat. They'd dismounted, and behind the horses she quickly restored her skirt into place. Making certain the waistband was straight, she raised her chin and smiled at the man welcoming her to his ranch.

"So good to have you here, ma'am. And Slocum, we can always use your gun. Did you see any Apaches?" Oglethorpe replaced his hat as Sandy shed Slocum's hat and tried to straighten her hair and his kerchief.

"Mostly the dead and their devastation," Slocum said, nodding to some of the cowboys who'd gathered around to hear his report.

"I saw one ranch woman and her daughter dead beside the road north of her schoolhouse. Another was a prospector full of arrows in the brush up at Chevron Springs. But there's either haystacks burning, or ranch houses, all the way down here from the stage stop in Apache Pass."

"You see any of them?"

Slocum shook his head. "Once we hid in some junipers for them to go on by us up there. All we did was hear them arguing while we were hidden. The horse I rode gave out carrying us double, and we caught these two horses running loose that the boys are putting up. Damn grateful to find them. My horse was run plumb out."

Sandy agreed.

"Well I have quarters for both of you," Oglethorpe said. "One of the maids will draw your baths, and you can wear some of my clothing, Slocum. I have a dress should fit you, ma'am."

"Thank you," she said, sounding grateful.

"There are some guest cabins at the side of the main house. Slocum can show you your room. You have number one and he has two. Bathwater will soon be there, and about nine this evening we can have supper in the main house."

"Very good, thanks," Slocum said and indicated to his companion that the way was up the flat rock steps to the next level.

He came a few steps behind her. "Oran is a very rich man. Polite and nice to me, and he will be to you as well. He has no wife. I never knew why not." He caught up beside her. "These room are well appointed."

She hugged her arms. "Good. But I'm just so pleased to be here in a safe place at last."

He opened the door to her room, and she went inside and agreed with him about the furnishings.

"Are you satisfied?" he asked her.

She drew in her breath. "If I can't sleep tonight—will you be available?"

"I will. Come over. I know today has been a chilling day for you. Sorry I was so rough on the start, but I was upset already."

"You never mentioned the dead woman and child beside the road to me."

"It was real tough on me to talk about it and not being able to settle it." He shook his head.

She turned, came back, and hugged him tight. In his ear, she whispered, "I have thought about you all day. This man had no reason, but he risked his own life to save me. He came back, rode his poor horse double, and saved my life. And that was another risk—the horse could have died had you not found those stray horses."

He wrapped his arms around her and they simply stood in one place.

"And you have no—roots—"

His whisker-bristled mouth closed on hers to silence her. Her arms quickly pressed her body against him. He felt her needs and regretted knowing that the bucket brigade of Mexican girls would soon be arriving with bathwater for them.

"Later," he said softly, and she backed up and nodded.

The knock on the door made him smile. "They have arrived."

He swung the door open and bowed. Then in Spanish he said, "Come right in, señoritas. The señora is ready. That is a lovely dress you brought for her. She is much grateful for what you are doing for her."

They giggled as if he were teasing them, while they poured the hot water in the copper tub and laid out towels, expensive soap, and a hairbrush for her.

She thanked them too and put the dress on the bed.

The last one out said, "You are next, Señor Slocum."

"Gracias." He closed the door and put his butt against it. "Until later."

"Yes." She smiled but looked close to tears. "I'll be fine. Thanks to you and our host."

"I better get over there in my place. They'll be right back. They're like a volunteer fire department bucket line."

In his room, he saw someone had brought his Winchester and saddlebags for him and put them by the bed. In a short while the five girls came back with hot water, towels, and clothing for him to wear.

The chubby one who was the leader stood with her back to the closed door. "You know what you must do to them for bringing you that hot water?"

He nodded. It was a tradition, and thank God they hadn't pulled it on him next door.

"Each one is a virgin and you must kiss each of them hard or we won't leave," she said, looking giddy. "They need some experience with a real man."

"I am all whiskered up," he whispered.

"We won't leave until you kiss each one of them."

He swept the first one up, her eyes wide open, and kissed her, feeling her small boobs under the thin material. "Thank you, my angel."

She staggered backward. Next number two—dark eyes wide open. He kissed her and felt the crown of her womanhood under the thin dress material at the bottom of her slight belly.

Next one, he squeezed her hard ass as he kissed her.

Then the last one was taller, and her blouse was open enough he decided he could reach in and squeeze a real boob. Her bare skin felt smooth as silk under his calloused hand. The small body of it was solid as a rock, and before the end, her tongue sought his mouth. She was ready or had already lost her maidenhood—no matter, it was all in fun.

The other girls swooned when they saw what he'd done to her. And he spanked her lightly on the ass going away.

"Great virgins you have there." He threw the leader kisses, and they left whispering and giggling, closing the door after themselves. The Pitch Fork could be a place to have real fun.

He had dried off from his bath when there was knock on his door. "Be right there."

"I'm sorry, were you still bathing?" she asked as if he might have been.

"No, but I still have to dress and shave."

"Don't bother to dress. I am not some willy-nilly girl that has not seen a man out of his clothing. Besides I can shave you."

His pants on, he opened the door and let her in. As she crossed the room, he studied the long blue silk gown she wore. "I won't argue about you doing that. You look quite lovely. Too nice to mess with a tramp."

"No, you're mistaken. This water is warm enough. She dipped some from his bathwater in a mug and made foam with a hog hairbrush. "You have a sharp razor?"

"In my saddlebags."

"Good. Sit in a chair over here." She put the mug down and searched in his saddlebags for his razor. When she found it, she went to where he sat on a ladder-back chair next to the mug on the dresser. He noticed her feet gliding across the floor. Maybe they could dance? She certainly looked like she'd be very talented at that.

She lathered his face and smiled. "I am over shaking, so I shouldn't cut you."

"Good thing!"

"Oh, Slocum, it has been such a tough day, I know for you as well." The blade slid through his beard stubble like a knife through soft butter. She frowned, impressed as she cleaned off the blade. "My comparisons to doing this for my late husband are all I have. He never owned a razor this sharp in his life. Whew. Was this instrument expensive?"

"I don't know. A woman in my past presented that to me."

"I bet you don't even know her name."

"Bet's on."

"Who was it?"

"Becky Oneida."

She quit shaving and laughed harder. "You made that up."

"No, she lives in Benton County, Arkansas, and owns a watermill there. I saved her from three shy-pokes who'd stopped there aiming to rape and rob her."

"You are serious?"

"Serious as I can be. I stopped there at the mill for directions to a fellow I'd been in the war with. I climbed the stairs to the open back door, and the mill was grinding corn so it was loud, I figured someone was inside watching the milling operation.

"Those three had her near stripped naked lying on her back on pile of gunnysacks. She wasn't letting her state of undress stop her none—she was fighting them like a wildcat.

"The only guy with his pants up went for a gun in his waistband."

She finished shaving the other cheek. "Go ahead with the story."

"Another who'd had his pants down, a pimply-faced kid, when he saw me, dove for his gun on the table. I'd warned them, and I shot him in the chest at point-blank range, in the midst of the billowing gun smoke. Then she used a sack knife she got hold of to stab the one on top trying to rape her." In reality she'd cut off his manhood and then in her rage cut his screaming throat—but Sandy didn't need to know about that part of the story

Careful-like, Sandy shaved his upper lip.

"That was one hell of a day. We laid them out after she got herself together, then we sent for the law, and a deputy came down, listened to her story, shook both our hands, and said, 'They deserved it. Case is closed. You can bury them.'"

"This was a real gift." And she wiped the soap off of the blade. "Did you ever find your friend from the war?"

"No, he'd gone west. I never saw or heard of him again."

She finished shaving the rest of his face and rinsed the razor. With a wet towel she cleaned away all the traces and inspected the job she'd done. She kissed him and he put her on his lap.

"A hell of a damn day. Tell me about yourself."

"I grew up on a Kansas farm. Went through the eighth grade in school. Later I went to two years of college in Manhattan after I passed an admissions test. My father wanted me to become a doctor. I wasn't sold on that idea, so I came home and married Franklin. Then he got shot in a cross fire during a bank robbery. I had known him growing up. I guess we had what you'd call a private friendship. I trusted him. We had swum naked at night when we were teens. We'd never done anything but kiss, and well maybe feel, until our wedding night. That event wasn't perfect, but we got better at it. I thought, anyway. On the day of the funeral I came to find out he had another woman, and two of her kids she claimed were his. I couldn't believe it. So I had a bigger letdown than simply being a widow that day. After all that happened, I simply had to leave Kansas. In a newspaper ad I found they needed a teacher here, and since I was a widow I qualified."

He kissed her, and he knew there was a fire inside of her banked for a big blaze. He closed his eyes—it would be hard to wait that long, but worth every minute for what he aimed to syphon from her.

"Should we go up there now?" She meant to the main house.

"We can, and be friendly."

She hugged his arm when he stood up to put on the borrowed shirt. "I am so grateful that you came by my school today."

He kissed her forehead and finished dressing. "That must have been hard finding out your dead husband had another wife across town, and he wasn't there to defend himself."

"It was the darkest day in my life. Worse even than today's scare."

What in the hell could he say? He'd caught something in her conversation about her saying they *got better at it*? Did she worry she wasn't good enough for him and that was why her husband went to find another woman?

They'd get it all ironed out—somehow. He shut the door behind them, and they walked side by side around to the front and entered the left side of the double doors that must have been ten feet tall.

Like the flooring in their rooms, the Mexican tile in the main house shone like glass. A woman in a very expensive dress greeted them like she had been waiting for them. She was short, with nice cleavage exposed and her hair all pinned up. She told them her name was Margareta and she was Oglethorpe's hostess.

This was a different woman than the one who had run his household Slocum's last time there. This woman wasn't as pretty as the one the year before, but she was very sweet and a better hostess. She showed them to the dining room and asked if they wanted a drink. She had everything. Slocum took a double Kentucky whiskey with a dash of water. Sandy chose a red wine.

Oglethorpe joined them, smiling and rubbing his hands together. "How did you get back in this country, Slocum?"

"Some guy named Dan Delight, who ranches down on the border, asked me to help stop some bad Mexicans who were robbing and raping women as well as rustling his cattle."

"Delight. Is his brand a Double D?"

"I think so. It was on the letter he sent me."

"I met him once at a cattlemen's protection meeting in Tucson. Short man, isn't he?"

"Yes. But he's a fist fighter and can whip a big man."

"Does he bite their legs?"

Sandy was laughing aloud by then.

"I'm not sure, but he laid out two men in a row when we were down in Mexico one time and he boxed in the ring against them."

"Sandy, your friend has had so many great adventures. You must get him to tell you about some of them."

"Thank you. I will."

The meal proved excellent. Margareta, who sat beside Slocum at the head of the table, rang a small bell and the help jumped through hoops like circus dogs. It amused him. A three-piece Mexican band—guitar, drums, and trumpet—played really great music, with "No Quarter Given" at the end.

"I am certain after today's escape you both are tired and ready for bed," the rancher said. "I expect the Apaches to try and storm this castle at sunup. May I invite you to join us then, *mi amigo*?"

"Wake me at five," Slocum said. "Or anytime you need me."

"I can have someone do that. *Gracias, senora*, so nice to meet you."

They thanked Margareta as well and went back to Sandy's room. Without lights on they kissed, standing past the locked doorway. She swiftly unbuttoned his shirt between them as their mouths sought each other. Then her hands massaged his hairy chest and the muscular cords of his belly.

Button by button he started to undo the back of her dress. She finally stopped him. "I can take it off now over my head. Lift it up. I'll help you."

"Good. I'd've been all night undoing them back there."

They laughed when the dress came off and she gently

laid it aside. Then, in the moonlight straining in the room's windows, she shed the slip. He saw her pear-shaped beasts and the slight rise of her belly that dove off between her legs into the patch of pubic hair. Busy kissing her standing up, with his finger he gently began feeling her clit. She moved her feet apart so he could edge the finger inside her vagina. Then she clutched him.

"Too fast?" he asked

"No, just right."

He swept her up and laid her on the bed. Then he undressed and joined her side by side on the sheet. Her hand on his side, she eased it downward and soon clutched his growing manhood. For a second at the squeeze of her fingers, her eyes flew open over her discovery.

With her breasts pressed to him, she sighed, "All I have ever had was my own experience as a wife. But yours is so much larger than his ever was. Oh, this will be wonderful." She shook her head fiercely then pressed her hips against him.

He rolled her over onto her back, and testing her with his two fingers, he decided she was lubricated enough. Next he climbed over between her legs and with his hand slowly inserted his great sword, which he followed with a few short strokes. Her legs wrapped and locked around his calves, he began pumping her with his stone-hard dick.

Her mouth open, she moaned, and her heat began to rise as his piston felt the muscles inside her and grew harder and larger. Catching her breath in gulps, she returned her action to his shaft. And they went further and further, until she half fainted.

Groggy sounding, she said. "I'm on fire. I'm so hot I'm on fire." Her breath came in gasps. He reached under her, gripped both cheeks of her butt, and then strained hard. His cum split wide open the head of his dick with its force. She sucked in her breath and seemed to faint away.

He never moved off of her. Braced above her on his hands and arms, he bent down and kissed her. Her opened eyes looked groggy, but pleased as well.

"Do it again?" she asked dreamily.

"Sure."

She hugged him tight. "Wonderful. I can see that you are heavenly good at this game."

He smiled at her. "Darling, you are wonderful too."

"Good. I've blamed and blamed my ineptness for him going to that other woman."

He kissed her on the mouth. "Not your fault. Darling, you are made for this too."

She hugged him and pressed her hard nipples into him. Their mouths soon began to feed off each other. His erection stiffened, and he went back to stroking her with the rigid stem, feeling her clit scratching the top of him going in and out. The nose of his tool was swollen skintight again, and the muscles inside her squeezed him, sending currents of pleasure to his brain. His breath grew harder and harder to catch. His hips ached, and the entire muscle structure that drove him in and out of her felt so bound up it might burst. Then he felt relief coming up the tubes. The action cramped the muscles in his ass, like two hot needles stuck in his butt. The explosion flew out the head of his dick and filled her cavity with cum.

She cried out and fainted in a heap. He smothered her with kisses, and, recovering, she hugged him real tight. "This was so, so good."

He got up to find a towel to take up any fluids leaking from her.

She put the towel under her and drew him back down.

"A little messy, but I can't tell you how l fretted over my body and my use of it being less than good enough for a real man."

He swept back the hair from her face and kissed her hard again. They lay on the bed and savored each other's nakedness. He tasted her nipples and toyed with them. She hugged his face to her when he got too serious.

"Here we are in the middle of nowhere," she said, "surrounded by bloodthirsty Apaches and having a honeymoon in another man's bed."

"Tonight it is your bed."

"I am so enthralled with you and your body. Also what it does to me. I want it to continue—"

"Let's simply enjoy the time we have together. I can't make any promises to you that it will last forever. But right now we have each other. Let's sip it like good wine and hope it lasts for the time we can be together."

"I will. But I could do it again and again—with you."

He moved in and kissed her. In no time they were back to being ready. She rose and soon straddled his erection in the starlit room. Easing herself down, she began the rise-and-drop on his stiff rod that made the bed ropes sing.

Heavens, he enjoyed her ways, and she took away the gravity of his existence, of being, as she said, *a drifter.*

In the morning , they went to breakfast with Margareta. A cheerful woman, she talked about things like the green-headed parrot she was teaching to talk. His name was Pablo. Slocum knew about the large flocks from Mexico that sought pinecones in the fall and flew clear to the Mogollon Rim some years to find them. They were also as common as pine trees in the desert high mountain islands like the Chiricahuas and Mount Graham. Many Apaches kept the parrots as pets.

"He learns words fast," Margareta said to them.

"Maybe when things return to normal, I can have one in my classroom. The children love animals, and a talking bird might be a good subject to discuss with them."

"Oh, he is such a baby."

"Where is Oran this morning?" Slocum asked.

"Oh, he and four guards rode to the border. He had some business down there."

"Do the men expect an attack from the Apaches?" he asked her. Her boss had told them he expected an attack that morning. Something must have changed his mind.

"No, the Apaches don't want to die fighting these cowboys who work for Señor Oglethorpe. They are different people than the Chiricahuas and the Jimenez from Mexico. Those savages were the ones that kept the big ranchers off their ranches for years up here in Sonora," Margareta said.

Slocum nodded, and thanked Margareta for breakfast. She said lunch would be at noon, and if they needed anything, to call on her. The two of them went back to their rooms.

At lunch Oran's foreman came into the main house and ate with them. "I have three men out scouting for signs of the Apaches this morning. I feel certain a company of buffalo soldiers will swing by here today or tomorrow. If you wish to leave, you can go to the fort with them."

"It is whatever Mrs. Brown desires to do," Slocum said.

She realized he expected an answer from her. "I doubt they will start school as long as this renegade problem is at hand. Do you wish to go see the man who asked for your help?"

"We can go see him if the Apaches have moved north."

"I should know where they are at by late afternoon," the foreman said.

"We can go after sundown and they won't bother us," Slocum suggested, and Sandy nodded that would be fine.

"I'll have those ponies you rode in shod, so you two will have a better outfit."

"I can do that," Slocum said.

"No, you're his guest. I have plenty of men standing around today."

"Thank you," Slocum said. "I'll return the favor someday."

"No worries about that. I know you'd have fought beside us if they had charged us."

"Very good. Margareta, we won't be here for supper tonight. I'll borrow a packhorse and a few items for us to travel with. After sundown we'll be on our way."

"I'll have that ready too," the tall Texan drawled. He nodded to Sandy, then Margareta when he excused himself.

When the two of them came out of the house, Slocum said to Sandy, "We should reach the Applegate Mine by tomorrow morning. We'll rest there tomorrow and then ride to the ranch headquarters the next night."

"Sounds good to me, since you said the Indians don't fight at night." She hugged him and bounced her hip off him. "You have me so charmed, I am not sure who I am. Or *where* I am even."

"Good." He kissed her temple and opened the door. "We better nap."

"Before or after the next chapter?"

That evening after the sunset and the first coyote howl, and after they had thanked Margareta, Oran still wasn't back yet. They quietly rode out the ranch gate and headed southwest, leading a packhorse behind. The outline of the towering Huachuca Mountains stood against the southern sky. They pushed westward until they hit the military trace. The stars were brilliant and the way easy, so by what Slocum considered to be near four A.M., they approached the Applegate Mine in the hills.

"Is that smell from a fire?" Sandy asked.

"I don't know."

From the top of the next rise, the smoke and smell were obvious. The entire setup had been burned to the ground, making squares of the foundation framing amid the glowing red ashes, the fire still licking the air above them.

"Were they attacked?" Sandy whispered.

Slocum nodded under the starlight, perplexed by the glowing remains of the mine operation buildings. His fist filled with his Colt revolver, and he told her to stay back with the packhorse. He hurried the gray to the base and saw several bodies facedown in the open.

"Anyone here?" he asked out loud. The smoke from the blaze was burning his nose and eyes as he wheeled his mare around. No answer. He hated to leave anyone there wounded, but he also was responsible for Sandy's safety. They'd better head for Patagonia. The village on Sonoita Creek was the closest settlement to the mine.

"What do you think happened?" she asked when he joined her.

"Apaches I guess. I've got no answer. Must have happened late yesterday. There is a small town close by. We better head there."

She nodded, and they rode off the mountain and went on west when they reached the wagon road. Slocum was on a tense alert leading the way. Dawn would soon be up and would free any Apaches of the gravity they felt about attacking in the dark. He scanned the junipers and brush on the hillsides and encouraged Sandy to push her horse faster. They dropped down into the draw that led to the village, and he decided then they might make it unscathed.

But at once two braves on horses charged them, coming out of hiding from a nearby dry wash. The air filled with war cries. Slocum saw them coming, and Sandy screamed.

The Colt rocked in his hand with a resulting thunder and a veil of gun smoke in his eyes. The shot took the one on the right off his horse. The second one's rifle must have jammed or misfired, and he'd dropped it.

Then the Apache drew a long knife from his belt and ran his mount hell-bent into Slocum's mare.

The collision threw the mare and Slocum into the sand. Somewhere in the impact, he lost his Colt. The mare's frantic effort to get herself up gave Slocum enough time to look for it. But there was no pistol in sight.

The Apache veered from his course to get at Slocum. With enraged, violent screams, he charged across the last short space to drive his knife into his enemy's heart. The day had come. Slocum had nothing but his bare hands, and he prepared for the last fight of his life.

The sharpened edge of the knife glinted off the high sun. Sharp enough to cut notepaper. The murderous brown eyes above him were intent on killing this white male.

An ear-shattering rifle shot rang out, and to Slocum's shock the shots kept coming. The knife-wielding Apache withered to the ground, struck several times by the smoking Winchester, the butt of which Sandy held against her hip. Even though it was empty, she kept levering the gun open and shut, and then the click of the firing pin was audible too.

He took the rifle by the barrel and removed it from her hands. She collapsed against his chest. The weapon slipped from his grip, and he hugged her, for she looked close to fainting.

"Oh my God, Slocum, I thought he would kill you."

"He would have, but you stopped him. You saved my life, girl."

"I had to do something. I'd shot a .22 like that gun. I had to run down the mare and get it out of your scabbard and struggle to get back with it. Oh, I am shaking all over. I never saw anyone that intent on anything like he was intent on killing you."

"He might have. You did the only thing that you could do. Stopped him. Are you all right?"

"I never killed anything before. Not even a chicken. My mother did that. But I gritted my teeth so hard my jaw is beginning to ache. I think I am fine now."

"I'll catch the horses," he said, sweeping up his Colt and holstering it. He'd also need to clean it. There would be lots of sand in its works.

She glanced back. "Should we bury them?"

"No. Let's ride on." He brushed the sand off the rifle. It would be okay, but when he caught the horses he'd have to reload it. Then clean it too later, because the bullets were corrosive.

The rifle jammed back in its scabbard, he spoke softly to the goosey mare. She stopped.

He gave the reins to her and then walked through the deep sand to catch Sandy's bay. Close calls—he'd had lots of them in his life, but that one—at the time even he thought he might make it to the big pasture afterward.

With her boosted in the saddle, he clapped her leg. "Let's get to Patagonia, girl."

She nodded. "I'm ready, Slocum, but I'm still shaking inside."

"Me too."

They rode off.

The many scattered wagons along the roads and streets told him that lots of refuges were already there. Slocum reined up under the mesquite trees in front of the one-sided business district crowded with wagons full of people's belongings. Obviously many ranch people had come in to seek safety. Children ran about. Strange dogs bristled at other newcomers.

A mustached man with a shotgun in hand greeted Slocum. "Howdy, mister."

Slocum looked over the situation and nodded. "Good morning. Are there any of the mine operation people here?"

"Did they attack the mine?" a big man of authority came forward and asked.

"Burned it to the ground. We were up there about two hours ago. Mrs. Brown was with me, so I could do little. I was concerned about her safety and we hurried down here."

With a grim look on his face, he shook his head. "None of them made it in here that I know about. I better get a posse together and go up there. They've raided several ranches we know about. I sent word to the fort to send some soldiers down here, but my man might not have gotten through."

"My name's Slocum. After I find a place for her to stay, I'll ride back with you."

"Thanks. I can use you. Not many men came in with their families, which is not good, but they had stock and their houses to try to protect. I can't believe they surprised Chuck Moore at the mine and wiped him out."

Slocum dismounted. "They damn sure did a smashing job of it. Every building was burned to the ground. Only a few minutes ago I shot one and she stopped the other one not two miles back up the road. So they are out there."

The man looked sad about the news concerning the mine and about their having been attacked so close. "I'll start gathering a posse."

"Are there any hotel rooms left?" Slocum asked.

"Yes, most of these ranch people here will camp out by their things."

Slocum agreed and thanked him, then turned to Sandy. "I'll get a room in the hotel for you, then put your horse in the livery. The marshal wants to go to the mine."

"I understand," she said.

After registering her for the room, they went to the livery and put up her horse and the packhorse. Slocum also secured a stall for his gray later. He gave Sandy ten dollars for expenses and kissed her on the cheek.

"Slocum, you be very careful today."

He agreed and said, "I should be back by dark."

"You be careful. That is what is important."

He winked at her. "Yes, ma'am."

Leading the gray up the street, he met another rancher, named Ward, and learned that the marshal's name was Gosbee—Harry Gosbee. Ward was an older man with silver hair and a mild way.

"I guess he asked you to be in the posse?" Ward said.

"Yes. We got here a few minutes ago. We were at the burned-out site about two hours ago. The mine structures were burned down, and several bodies were strewn about—I had Mrs. Brown with me and couldn't risk stopping that close to dawn. And we were attacked by two Apaches not two miles from here."

"Well, my lands." Ward made a hard face. "You were sure lucky and so was she. Be a shame if they killed everyone up there."

Slocum agreed.

In a short time, the posse of twelve men rode for the Applegate Mine, led by Marshal Gosbee. It took them an hour and a half at a hard trot to reach the disaster scene, with no sighting of any Apaches. The two dead ones had been gathered by the others. The sight of the mine sickened Slocum. People he had known were dead. The posse covered the corpses under blankets the marshal had brought along.

Several men found picks and shovels in the mine to begin digging graves. Not one soul was found alive. Ten dead men, including the mine superintendent John Harness, whose body was found partially burned where he'd died gun in hand, defending the operation.

Slocum knew him well. A hardworking, tough individual who had managed the operation successfully for a number of years. In the remains of the office they found the great safe open; papers inside had been burned, but there was no gold in it.

"Damn Apaches never stole gold before," Gosbee said to Slocum.

"They may have found it would buy rifles from unscrupulous dealers in Mexico and even up here."

Gosbee frowned at him. "That makes sense. But who taught them that?"

"They can see people buying things, from whiskey to groceries, with gold dust and not much of it."

"Two and two, it makes sense. I can't hardly believe it, but I guess they ain't that dumb not to find out."

"What's wrong?" Ward asked, joining them in the ashes of the office.

"We think they took the free gold he kept in his safe."

"Ain't that something?" Ward shook his head. "They ain't the durn fools you think they are."

Gosbee agreed with a nod. "Now where will they spend it?"

"That's a thousand-dollar question." Slocum chuckled over his own words. Who would sell them arms? No telling, but probably some Mexican bandits south of the border. For the moment, he was anxious to get back to Mrs. Brown.

"Where in the hell is the army at?" Gosbee looked around and shook his head in disgust. "We've got thousands of troops stationed down here, and these damn scoundrels run around them and then get away."

The list of dead men's names completed, they began lowering bodies into the fresh graves. It had been hard work in the dry earth to dig the graves deep enough. The men had even used some blasting sticks to help them loosen the caliche soil. At last the ten corpses had been laid to rest, and with their hats taken off, the men of the posse listened to some kind words that were said for the departed souls. Amen.

They saddled up and rode back. On the road a troop of buffalo soldiers on horseback met them. A white officer led them and halted the column.

"You're too damn late," Gosbee shouted at the officer. "They killed everyone at the Applegate Mine last night. They killed everyone and stole the superintendent's free gold out of the safe before they burned the place down."

"What did they need gold for?" the lieutenant asked.

"To buy more damn guns." Grosbee jerked his horse around. "You need to find these killers and round them up."

"Any signs over there at the mine?"

"I doubt it."

"What 'bout the dead?"

"Buried."

"What will happen to the mine now?"

"I guess Harness's family will decide."

The posse rode on, and the army followed them into town. It was late afternoon. Slocum had had little to eat all day, so once he had the gray in the stables, he gathered Mrs. Brown and they went to a local café for supper.

"Tough day?" she asked, seated across from him.

"A very tough one. I liked the man who managed the mine. He was a good person."

"What will the army do about it?"

"Ride around and look for the wind."

She smiled at him. "They can't chase them down?"

"No. You need a fox to catch a fox. They don't have enough Apache scouts working for them. These other tribes they use for scouts are not much help in tracking down an Apache."

"Do they know that?"

"Yes, but it is hard to get the tribesmen to work against their brothers."

"What will we do?"

"I need to go meet with this man who asked me to come help him. Then I can take you back—maybe you can get started teaching next week."

"What will the army do about the renegades?"

"Keep chasing them."

"Oh, that is good news."

He agreed.

The waiter brought them their suppers of roast beef, mashed potatoes, gravy, and green beans, plus sourdough bread and butter. He sipped his hot coffee and nodded to her. "The meal looks very good for such an isolated place."

"Very good," she said after tasting the potatoes and gravy.

"You spoke about the Apaches learning gold could buy things."

"Yes. They took the free gold Harness kept in the safe. Might be quite a lot of gold if we knew the amount they had on hand. Of course the books were burned and all of them were killed. So only the Apaches know how much was there."

"This rancher that called for your help lives near here?"

"Yes, west of here about ten miles. I'll go see what his problem is in the morning and then be back here tomorrow afternoon."

"Can we go back to the room after this?" she asked hesitantly.

He smiled. "Sure."

"Good," she said, sounding relieved.

Back at her room, they took a quick trip to the bed. Then he sat up on his butt with his back to the headboard. She lay with her head resting in his lap, basking in the last sundown's red glare coming in the hotel room window. Idly, he coiled her hair on his fingers and wondered how other people he knew in this country had survived the widespread attacks.

"What comes next?"

"You stay here a day or so. I am going to go and check on Dan. I'll be back or be certain the marshal gets you back home safely."

"That sounds bad."

"Hey, I live on the knife's edge all the time. I damn sure plan to be back. You sit tight. This is as safe as any place I know for you to be, save the fort."

She reached up and pulled his face down. "Could we stop the clock? And you and I stay here forever?"

"About dark I am going to saddle up and go see him. I'll be back. You are safer here than anywhere I know save the fort—and that's a long ride over there. Those Apaches won't strike this town. There are too many guns here. You need some money?"

"No, you left me plenty."

"Well all right."

"I hate for you to go. They may kill you."

"It happens."

"Oh, all right, get yourself killed and what will I do?"

"Darling, with a body like yours, all you have to do is cross the room."

She scowled at him. "You don't know. You aren't a woman whose husband left her for a wench. If I am so attractive, why did he mess with her?"

"Darling, if I knew that answer I could write a book on it and get rich. Trust me, you are beautiful and make a hot lover—his preferences I don't know anything about. Some guys run around on their wives 'cause they're insecure and that makes them feel big. But he was plain stupid."

She rose up on her knees, threw her arms around his neck, and smothered him with kisses. Aw, hell, then they had to have sex again.

Dan Delight should be at his ranch when Slocum got there before daylight. His gray mare out of the livery, he left in twilight, headed west down the creek. His one hand on his cleaned Colt butt and the other on the reins, he cranked his head around a lot, thinking the thick brush and willow might hold a bloodthirsty Apache.

He came out in some open, starlit grassy lands and swung south. The land was all grass, with a few century plant stalks here and there. Some old Apache buck had said that his people lived where the century plant grew and flowered once in fifty years, and then died.

They dug up the roots of them and the squaws made beer. The buck had had some, but he preferred the real white man's beer. The Apaches' corn beer wasn't much better. But a pint of good whiskey could buy an Apache's wife for one night. Whew, they loved that.

By dawn Slocum was approaching the ranch, and before the sun rose over the Huachuca Mountains to the east, he could see some lights at the house. That was Dan's place.

He kicked the mare out in a long lope and headed there. No sign of any Apaches. He felt relieved, and closer he let out a shout. "White man coming. Don't shoot."

The rifle-bearing cowboy was laughing when he reached him. "What the hell are you doing out here?"

He stepped off the mare and shook his hand. "My name's Slocum. What's yours?"

"Garby, Garby Hanks, glad to meet'cha Slocum."

"Where's the boss man?"

"Coming. Hell, man, you came at a tough time." Slocum's shorter friend Dan came bailing out of the lighted door of the ranch house. "Good to see you got here in one piece. These Apaches have gone tonto bronco, ain't they?"

Dan meant *crazy wild*. A term that Slocum had heard all his life in the border country, for someone who went on a shooting drunk spree. He agreed and Dan showed him inside. "Get some breakfast. Goldie, your buddy's here."

Goldie looked up. A tall blond woman with braids piled on her head, large boobs, and a thick waist in a dress and apron. She still was a looker. At one time she had commanded high prices for turning tricks with a john. But she'd left that all behind to cook for Dan's outfit and raise hell with him and his cowboys.

"Gawdamn, Slocum." She tackled him. Then she hugged him tight enough to squeeze the air out of him and French-kissed him. Everyone close by whopped, and someone hollered. "She's got her one to ride now, boys."

Not embarrassed a bit, she told them, "By God, boys, you can't beat this guy in bed. If you were as good as him, you wouldn't have to punch cows another day. My heavens how long has it been since we were together?" she asked Slocum.

"A couple of years anyway."

"Yeah, me and Shorty and you were down there in Sonora together."

She was the only person alive who could call Dan that and live. He winked at her. One thing Slocum observed, she still wore good-smelling perfume, and no doubt could still break the ropes under the mattress when she got wound up.

"Them crazy red devils've lost their minds, haven't they?" she asked. "Must be eating them mushrooms that make them hallucinate, huh?"

"They are bad. Burned the Applegate Mine buildings

and killed ten men over there. I rescued a schoolmarm over near Apache Pass. We made it to Patagonia. And we even had a scrap with two of them before we got there. I left her in town. Lots of ranch families are staying there."

"Aw, you rescued her, my ass. You won't ever change. But I bet she appreciated that."

"Feed this man," Dan said. "The rest of your business with him can wait till dark. He must be starved."

"I will. I will. I'm just excited to see him. Don't he look good?"

"Depends what you want him for. I want him to help me stop these bloody Mexican raiders. You've got other purposes for him."

Slocum took a seat on the closest bench, and Goldie brought him a heaping plate of scrambled eggs, fried side meat, German potatoes, biscuits, gravy, butter, prickly pear jelly, and peach jam. Topped that with coffee and a slab of her own carrot cake.

"Ah hell, Goldie, you're spoiling him."

"I'll have you know I spoil all of you peckerwoods." She waved her index finger at all of them around the circle. "So there."

Dan slid in on the other side of Slocum. "His name is Gomez. Raul Gomez. He's an outlaw that even the Federales go around. You savvy—he either pays them or their bosses. But he's a real mean, sorry sumbitch. At any rate the authorities down there don't mess with him and his crowd."

"Is he selling the cattle he's taking in Mexico?"

"I'm not sure of much of anything. These boys of mine could fight a circle saw, but them banditos are tough too."

"Have you met them head-on yet?" Slocum asked him.

"Yes, we broke up the attempt they made to drive off several head. It ain't only cattle rustling. They raped Johnny Boyd's poor wife Lisa until she's lost her mind."

"Dan's not lying. That poor woman sits in a rocker all day and mumbles and screams out loud, 'Don't fuck me!'" Goldie shook her head in disgust. "She ain't the only one. Others never reported it."

"They raped some school-age girls at the Cone place," Dan said. "And one of them bastards killed a four-year-old boy. This Gomez is a bad deal and has got to be stopped."

"When you headed them off, did you do any good?"

"No. It was a running gun battle. But I figure that only pissed Gomez off and he'd sure come back loaded for bear the next time he tried to raid us."

"He has to have a big beef market down there, you reckon?"

"I don't know. He had lots of cattle when we ran them off, and we got most of ours back."

"How many?"

"They had close to a hundred head in the bunch when we jumped them. We shot four of them and wounded some more. But they got most of their men back and ran down south again."

"Must have been some running gunfight."

"It turned into a running one once we got them on the go. We chased them way down into Mexico. We were taking casualties on his men. Until I figured they might lead us into a trap down there and we hauled our asses back home."

Slocum considered that. "There's been no more action from them since then?"

"No, but the Apaches went on the rampage all over up here right after that. We figured that's keeping them home."

"This guy must have a market somewhere. Cattle in Mexico are cheap and no big place to sell many at one time. So why steal so many unless someone wanted to buy them?"

"Old man Clanton has all the markets over here sewed up. He steals half of his in Mexico to fill his orders."

Slocum knew all about the Clantons and their dealings. Gomez might be selling them to him all right.

Goldie refilled their cups and gave Slocum a slight bump with her butt. "These men are just starting to heal up from that scrap. It was blood and bandages around here for six weeks."

Slocum nodded and said, "The only way to stop him is to take the war to him. You kill him or he kills you. As long as he's down there running a gang, he'll be right back up here raiding stock and raping innocent women again. You got better eating stock than those brush-eating Corrientes that are south of him, so why not steal your white-faced and roan cattle?"

"They are better eating anyway. I'll get ten more tough guys and we can go armed to the teeth. Think we can whip them."

"You may have to fight the Federales if you go down there."

"How can we duck them? I only want Gomez's head on a stake."

Slocum nodded. "You just have to take that chance and be on the lookout for them."

"I have my belly full of these bastards. I'll go find me a dozen more men. Can you wait a few weeks?"

"I can, but remember this. You are taking a big chance tangling with politics in Mexico."

"I damn sure intend to stop this Gomez once and for all."

Slocum nodded and stretched out his legs under the table. "You'll need lots of answers about your enemy."

"What do you mean?"

"Have you ever scouted his fortress or his army?"

"No." Dan looked hard at him.

"I mean, you must find out some of his strengths and weaknesses. You can't just ride down there and start shooting.

If you intend to make a raid on him, you have to know what the hell you are going up against. Where his belly is most exposed at."

"How will I do that?"

"Let me slip down there and look it over. Hell, you might not have enough men or don't need that many."

"They'd kill you."

"Hell, others have tried doing that. I'm still here. I think I can infiltrate them. Figure out their points of strength."

"What will that cost?"

"My expenses."

"What do you think that will be?"

"A couple hundred I'd guess."

"I don't want you dead."

"Who'd cry?"

"Damn it, this ain't a suicide run, is it?"

"No." Slocum shook his head.

"When do I go look for your corpse?"

"If you don't get a telegram or me back from there in six weeks."

"Damn, I don't want you killed."

"I want a Mexican saddle, a brown horse, no brand, a serape, some Mexican blankets for a bedroll, some old knee-high boots, a vest, and some big-roweled spurs."

"When are you going down there?"

He considered the question. "In the morning."

Dan shook his head. "Damn, I'll have to get busy to find all that crap."

"Good. I'm leaving at sunup."

Dan stood up and sent his men off to get all the things he listed for them to find. "Get a move on you."

Then his concerned-looking buddy turned back to Slocum. "Get some sleep. You haven't had much lately. They will have all this stuff for you here tonight."

"Fine." Slocum sipped on the rich coffee.

Goldie was gathering dishes as everyone else started to leave. In a low voice, she said, "Go upstairs. First room on the right. They'll all be gone, but for a few clowns on guard duty. I won't be more than a few shakes of a lamb's tail getting up there."

"Fine," he said, agreeing to his sentence in bed with her. How long since they'd had an affair? Maybe four years, but it was in Mexico then. Goldie was a pleaser of men in bed; she knew how to do it right.

He went upstairs and looked out the second-story window at the river headed north for the Gila. The Santa Cruz wound through all the mission country in southern Arizona and even passed Tucson headed to join the Gila. Giant cottonwoods lined the small river, and it irrigated lots of places on its route. Dan had several fields where he raised crops and hay.

Taking his time at undressing, Slocum listened to the variety of birds that sought the tall yard trees for protection and fed on the ground. Every kind of bird was there, and in the winter more joined them. He hung his vest, six-gun, and holster on the back of the ladder-back wooden chair. Took off his boots next and socks, then his three-button shirt came off over his head. He was down to his waist overalls and had unbuckled the belt when Goldie came rushing into the room out of breath.

"You are getting slow—I can recall you getting stripped in no time to climb on me when I worked for Lady Bird Halman. You remember that? It was up in Silver City, New Mexico. God, I won't ever forget that time. I did a double take at your pecker and thought to myself you'd rip me in two with it. Oh, I still can remember you working me over." She had her britches off and was unbuttoning the dress she wore over them. Her breasts popped out, capped with dollar-size nipples, and soon the rest of the big gal's full body was shining in the room's bright light.

"Well I was a size or two smaller back then, but you get more to love this way. Damn it is good to have you here. I had a bad itching, and you can fix that."

He twisted her around and kissed her. Her mouth was as sweet and wet as a fresh watermelon. And brother, she could still kiss and get a guy going.

Afterward she said, "Oh, baby, I think it was better today than ever." She was trying to get the loose hair out of her face with her fingers. He was braced on his arms over her.

"You through for the day?" he asked.

"Hell yes."

So they did it again and then he took a nap.

3

By dark his items of clothing were there: a pair of leather pants that string-tied in the front; a white cotton shirt, hand-woven; knee-high soft boots that fit him fine; and a vest made from tanned sheepskin with leather on the outside, rough-stitched like some woman in camp must have sewed the two pockets on it. There were also two bandoliers to wear crisscross on his chest—.50-caliber cartridges. The tube-fed Spencer repeating rifle looked to be in perfect condition. He had used one enough in the war to know that when the action was tight they shot well.

There was a serape to wear over his clothes for warmth, and some fine goat-skin gloves, two pair of them, plus some real Mexican-looking saddlebags, with powder and balls for his .44. Then he saw the extra cylinders.

"We got you a good .44 Remington. You can load and exchange those cylinders easier in it than in a Colt," Dan said.

Slocum agreed.

The sombrero was an expensive one, but it had been worn before, he discovered as he put it on.

One cowboy could not resist and gave a *wha-hoo*.

Dan frowned at him. "This business is all secret. Your life may depend on what he finds out down there."

The guy nodded and sat back down.

There was some silver trim on the holster and gun belt with the large buckle. When Slocum tried it on and it fit, he nodded. "Fine."

Then he sat down and tried on the large rowel spurs they had for him. They clunked like church bells when he walked around in them. "You all did a helluva good job."

There was also a large knife that you wore in a harness under your clothes, and you could reach back at your collar, draw it, and throw it. Another fit in his boot top, and a .30-caliber derringer went inside his vest.

Plus a dozen sticks of blasting powder, loaded, carefully wrapped with long fuses, to place in his saddlebags. Also a leather container to hold the rifle tubes tied on the saddle. What hadn't they found for him?

"You can cut the fuses to size very easy," Dan said.

Slocum agreed.

"Here's the money belt, three hundred, most of it is Mexican money."

Goldie brought him a silk black kerchief and tied it around his neck, then kissed him. The men all laughed.

"We found a good high-headed, pacing horse too." Dan chuckled. "No brand on him."

"Good, you hombres stay out of my way." They all laughed.

He carried the clothing upstairs and redressed. He found he'd need to practice before he could draw the knife from the harness behind his back and make a smooth move with it. He finished dressing and decided that in a few days he'd be comfortable wearing it all. Before the moon rose, he left the ranch and rode to Patagonia to see Saundra. He knew his costume would scare her unless she heard his voice first. The pacing horse was high-headed, but he made real good time crossing the rolling country going back to Patagonia. Riding this horse was another thing he'd have to get used to. Nothing wrong using him as a traveling horse, but he preferred a ranch horse for himself.

He arrived midday and hitched Pancho to the rack before taking a seat on a bench and hoping Sandy would leave the hotel and he could see her. He wrote a note to her finally and had a young boy deliver it to the desk clerk.

He came back to Slocum.

"Señor, he said he would take it to her room."

"Gracias." He paid the boy another dime.

The freckle-faced youth asked, "Any more messages you need delivered?"

He shook his head.

"You need me, I'm Henry. Just whistle and I'll come."

"Sure."

The young boy skipped off with two dimes in his fist— no doubt for the candy counter. Slocum looked up and saw Sandy searching for him.

She soon stopped before him, but not looking at him. "What's wrong?" she asked.

"I'm going to Mexico and try to learn about some outlaws. Can you get a ride back to your school if I'm not back in time?"

"When will the Apache threat be over?"

"Soon, I suppose. Do you need money to stay here?"

"No, I have enough. When will you come back?"

"I'm not certain. I hate to leave—"

He was silent for some passing ladies, then began again, "I hate to leave you here."

"I can manage. I hate that we can't be together."

"Things happen. If I am ever near your schoolhouse, can I come by?"

She nodded. "Yes—do. I must go now. Be very careful."

"I will."

After she left, he rose, then unhitched and mounted Pancho. He rode out of the jam-packed town still full of folks waiting for word they could go safely home. It was straining the town's facilities. But Slocum knew there was no immediate answer to the problems of overcrowding.

He rode across the border to a small village, looking for information about Gomez. In a cantina he lounged with his chair to the wall, and a skinny *puta* came by and tried to coax him into paying her for her ass.

"I am young and I can entertain you in bed, *mi amigo*."

"Oh, I don't think so."

"No, no. I can make you a grand stallion or you don't have to pay me."

"What is your name?" His attention was hard on two men who had just come into the cantina. They looked like banditos, or at least they swaggered into the place like bullies who owned it.

The bartender greeted them, and it was obvious he did not know them. They told him they were new in the village and asked if he had any pretty *putas*. He said there were some in there.

The biggest man rested his elbows on the bar and gazed around the room like he was surveying the crowd of mostly peons in white clothing, heads down, not wanting any wrath from this man.

"Who made this beer?" the second man asked, spitting out a mouthful on the dirt floor. "This is too bad to serve to the public." He was a bulldog, shorter than his compadre.

"What do you say, Ringo? Should we shoot this *bastardo* for serving us horse piss?"

"That is the only beer I can buy, señor."

Slocum was still thinking on him calling his partner Ringo. There was a Johnny-come-lately at Tombstone went by that name, but he was a Texas cowboy who was handy with a gun. He was a gringo. This man must have taken his name to impress crowds like this one. What was the bulldog's name?

"*Cristo*, I don't know what to do. Kill him for keeping such ugly *putas* in here or poisoning you."

He grabbed a seated peon by a fistful of his shirt. Then he raised him up and asked him in his face, "How do you vote, *mi amigo*?"

"I no vote, señor."

The big man threw him down on the floor and kicked him in the ass, "Get the hell out of here then. You worthless piece of shit." The young man, hardly more than a boy, rushed out the swinging doors and was gone.

"I should have shot him in the ass, huh?"

Ringo approached another table, right next to the last one. When he moved to the next one, those at the first table got up and ran out the door. His haughty laughter rang out. "They have no dicks. No stallion in them. You have a big dick?"

The pale-faced man he had asked shook his head. "No, señor."

"What are you, a pussy?"

The man shook his head.

"I think it is time for you two to leave." Slocum's voice was low but audible.

He quietly told the girl to get aside. Then he rose slow-like and hitched his gun belt in place. "You don't want that old man, you want me."

"Huh? What did you say?" The *pistolero* blinked in disbelief at him.

"He said he wanted you, Ringo," Bulldog said with an evil grin.

"What's your name?" Ringo gave him a head toss.

"My name is not important. You, sir, are a bully. I think you should get on your horse and ride away from this village. These people are gentle people. They have no weapons, how can they fight you? They can't, and you punish men who are gentle men. Load your asses up and go. Otherwise this cannot end peacefully, like things here do every day when folks like you aren't here harassing people."

"You must be a *pistolero*. You are well armed."

"I am the man who challenged you to either fight me or leave."

"Oh, I see you want to fight with me."

"No, you don't want that."

"Why not?"

"What would your mother think of you in those clothes all bloody in a cheap coffin?"

"My mother is a whore in Juárez. She wouldn't care anything about seeing *you* dead."

Then the bartender put a snare around Bulldog's neck and had him with his back pulled hard to the bar. "Go ahead, señor. I didn't want him to try anything."

"Ah, Ringo, it is your last chance to get on your horse and ride away—alive."

Bulldog made growling sounds in his throat, trying to get his fingers under the noose choking him. He was backed over the top of the bar by the rawhide tool.

"Be calm, *mi amigo*. I will kill that bartender that has you now after I kill this gringo in men's clothing."

Ringo went for his gun, in slow motion to Slocum, whose pistol blasted a large cloud of gun smoke even before Ringo's pistol was fully cocked. The bullet went straight into his heart. In the next moment, Ringo's eyes widened in disbelief. He staggered, then fell down dead on the dirt floor.

But it was the sounds of Bulldog being strangled to death by the bartender that made Slocum sick to his stomach. Finally the bartender's assistant reached over and cut the big man's throat with a large-blade carving knife. No more gasping. Blood flew everywhere. The bartender let go of the noose, and Bulldog's body slumped on the floor. His left leg kicked in his dying reactions.

"Give me a glass of that beer," Slocum said. "Who cleans up in here?"

The bartender, with the beer, said, "All of us are so grateful to be rid of them. *Gracias, amigo.* Drink all the beer you wish."

"Come, my girlfriend. The smoke is too bad to stay in here. Where is your hammock at?"

She came skipping across the room and took his arm. "I will show you."

"Don't charge him either," the bartender said after her.

She shook her head. "I wasn't going to anyway."

Out of the batwing doors into the blinding sun, she took his arm, and they stopped to get his pacing horse to lead along with them.

"Where will you go next?"

"We can talk about that later. How far is your place?"

"Just a short ways. Why?"

"Is it far enough that we are going to ride this horse?"

"Oh, no. See that jacal on this hill? That is my casa."

"How did you get that nice of a place?"

"A woman and her three children died in there after a mad dog bit them. They died a horrible death. There was nothing anyone could do for them. People said their maddening screams were even in the adobe walls. I have never heard them."

"Good. I hate screams too."

"You never told me your home?"

"Where I sleep? Anywhere I lay down."

"Let's put him in the corral out back and unsaddle him. There is some hay. I want to learn all about you." She patted the arm she held. "You are a powerful man. Those men were killers who came by here often and scared the villagers. Me too."

"I am only going to stay one night."

"You are on a mission, no?"

"You could call it that. How did you know I had one?"

"I guessed it. At times it gets too hot to sleep on the ground. A hammock is nice if you don't fall out." She laughed. "Me and a customer did that one night in the middle of our business." With a laugh out loud, she hid her face on his sleeve. "We were too wild, huh?"

"Too wild is right." At her corral he unsaddled Pancho and put him in the pen. Grateful to have the saddle off, he rolled in the dust and wiggled on his back to stop the itching or whatever. They went to her adobe casa. A tattered bottom blanket was the door, and the south wind flowed through the place, surprisingly cool.

She shed her dress over her head. That was all she'd had on. He hung his gun belt rebuckled on a chair's back where it would be handy.

"You have no wife or children?" she asked.

"No."

She shook her head at his answer and then hung his vest on the wall. He removed his sombrero to place it on the other side of the chair's back, then she made him sit on the seat and pulled off his tall rawhide boots. He decided that perhaps she was being slow and deliberate in undressing him to make the evening with him pass more slowly, but he was bone-tired and she did not impress him.

When at last she had him buck naked, she asked, "Hammock or pallet?"

"Listen, I am too tired to make love to you. Let me sleep in the hammock."

She waved her finger at him. "If you fall out, don't be mad at me."

"I won't."

She acted pissed, but she'd get over it.

When he awoke, he gave her money to go buy them supper from a street vendor. She wiggled on her dress and ran off to find food. He went and watered his horse, then stopped to look at the array of stars. He wondered if the Apache business was about over and if Sandy could go back safely to her schoolhouse.

He and the skinny one ate the rich chunks of browned beef, onions, and sweet peppers, wrapped in large snowy flour tortillas, while seated cross-legged on a blanket on the floor.

"I told her I had a gringo who might not like her hot peppers."

He shrugged between bites. "Some are fine, but hot-hot is too much. You did good."

"Where will you go next?"

"I look for a bandito named Gomez."

Her eyes flew open and she about choked on her food. Huffing for air, she shook the tortilla in her hand at him. "Oh, he is a killer and madman. Don't go there. He will kill you." Tears ran down her face. "He is a mean sumbitch and his men are meaner than tigers. Oh, please don't go down there."

"Where does he live?"

"On a large hacienda south of St. Barnabas. Do you want to go dance or stay here?"

"Good," he said, watching her slither the dress up, first exposing her bird legs. Then the candlelight twinkled on his sight of her crotch and the patch of black pubic hair. Soon she showed him the deep navel in the brown skin of her stomach and then moved upward to expose her small, proud, pointed boobs, and then the dress was off over her head and short hair. Nice scenery to view.

"Girl, you are very sweet. I don't dislike you, but I have business down here to tend to, so maybe another time or place."

"Are you leaving me?" she asked in shocked disbelief.

"Yes."

He left the skinny one with some money that she first refused, but he made her take it. Then he rode off on the pacing horse. To go directly to the village near Gomez would be foolish. He needed to make a more casual ride, as if he was lost or wandering.

He left the main road, stopping to talk to a wood gatherer with a string of heavily laden burros, who told him about some hot springs across a small mountain range. He called the springs a good place to soak and get the pains out of his body. The trail was steep, but Slocum's horse was sure-footed and carried him over the pass. There he stopped to let the horse breathe, and the cooling wind swept his face.

The distant green cottonwoods told him the springs were down there. The discomfort of his tight back muscles could hardly wait for a few hours in the springs. He rode off the mountain to a spot under the towering, gnarled trunks of the cottonwoods. Several people were bathing in the obviously warm water—Indios who did not care if he saw them naked and who went on as if he was one of them passing through. Several pregnant women nodded to him. Some were close to the last stages.

To be by himself, he went on farther, to where a steaming spring fed the stream. He hobbled the horse and undressed, leaving his gun and holster close by. Wading into the hot water, he decided his body would not cook in it. He sat down up to his neck and let the fumes go up his dry nose and the hot water flow by him. The charge from the heat made him shut his eyes and savor the relief coming from being loosened up.

"Señor! Señor!" He rose some to see what was the matter.

It was a teenage girl on the road waving at him.

"What's wrong?" he asked.

"My mother is trying to have a baby. We need help," she shouted.

"You go back and hold her hand. I'll get dressed and come see what I can do."

"Gracias, gracias."

"Go." He waved her to go back before he rose naked from the water.

When he was satisfied she'd gone, he waded out, dried, and put on his clothes and gun belt. He caught up to his horse and unhobbled him, then rode back to where the half-dressed women were all crowded around one lying on a blanket.

He dismounted and cleared his throat so they knew he was there, and that separated the concerned onlookers. When they let him through the crowd, he dropped on his knees beside the woman on the ground. The small woman's belly looked like a mountain on top of her.

"Is the baby coming?" he asked.

"Trying to." She strained and made a pained grimace at her effort. A girl was trying to pat dry with a cloth the beads of sweat on her face.

He moved to be below her, where he could look at the delivery point between her legs. How was it coming? He

knew the danger was the baby coming feet-first. But he'd
never turned a baby around in a woman's womb either.

"Bring me some soap and water to wash my hands."

"*Sí.*"

She moaned in pain and her raised legs rocked from side
to side. He wished he could do more. A doctor had told him
that giving such women painkillers would make them stop
pushing hard enough. If he'd not heard that, he'd have given
her some laudanum.

"Be easy. We will bring him out. Be brave. What is her
name?"

"Lucille."

Water arrived. He washed his hands and dried them on
a clean towel. Then he moved in close and told Lucille that
he had to feel for the baby. She nodded and looked paler
than a few minutes before. His fingers probed her, and she
moved as if his action made her uncomfortable. He felt nothing. Using one hand down on the blanket to balance himself,
he slowly worked his folded other hand inside her. It must
have pained her, but he had to know the baby's position even
if he couldn't flip it over.

The women around him were moaning and clucking
when he felt what he thought was the baby's head. Good.
And then he drew his hand out, washed it in the pan they
handed him, and dried it on the towel.

"Push, Lucille. He will come out. Strain harder."

He kept coaching her and realized that the black spot he
was seeing was the baby's hair.

"Come on, push harder." He kept encouraging her until
the skull appeared and Slocum tried to help her, and soon
cradled the baby's head. Shoulders came next, and he helped
one out, then the other, in the leaf-filtered daylight. And then
the baby came faster, until he held him by his heels and
slapped his butt to start him breathing.

The baby's first cries made Slocum drop on his knees, and the women around him cheered.

"Lucille, he's a boy." He set him down on a clean blanket, cut the cord, and tied it off before he handed her the small brown boy. On his feet, he washed his hands again and stood back to dry them.

"*Gracias, señor.*" The woman was older than the others and taller than most Latin women, with a swollen willowy figure. Slocum decided that she might be pregnant herself.

"May I ask what brings you here?" she said with a smile.

"A wood cutter said these springs healed him. I wanted to help my back. I have been bucked off too many times."

"Then since you have no cook, you should come to my camp for supper."

"No problem with that. Is your husband here?"

"No." She shook her head. "He is dead. My name is Lupe."

"Slocum is mine. I am sorry I asked."

"No, he was killed by bandits. A short while ago."

"And that is his baby?" He nodded toward her belly.

"Yes, that is his baby. It will be how I will remember him."

Slocum agreed. "Where is your camp?"

She made a wave. "Beyond where they say you were bathing."

"I can find it. I'm going back to soak some more in the water. No more births today?"

She smiled and shook her head. "You did well. You can deliver mine in four months."

"I won't be close, I fear."

"*Gracias* for your work today. Wait—the mother wants to thank you."

He knelt beside her and the baby boy suckling on her breast. "What did you call him?"

"What is your name?"

"John."

"He will be Juan then. Come here, I want to kiss you for helping him get here."

He dropped on his knees and she kissed him and whispered, "God be with you, hombre."

With a nod he left her.

Slocum went back to his spot and hobbled the horse again. Unsaddled and undressed, he waded out in the stream and sat down at last once more in the heated water.

He saw Lupe's head held high coming above the willows. Somehow he had expected her to make an appearance at his soaking. No matter—she was an attractive woman and he was by himself.

"Do you accept company?" she asked

"Oh, yes. Why are all these women here?"

"Oh, they come for a saint's holiday."

"That's enough," he said, not really interested in the details and giving her a head toss to come on.

She was a neat-looking woman without her clothes. Pear-shaped breasts that looked a little swollen to him. The slight bulge of her belly was noticeable as she entered the water, but it was a sweet enough picture to make him grateful for her company.

"I have no modesty with you today. I saw how you go to that woman's aid, and I would have trust in you to deliver mine."

"Get a midwife or a medical doctor. I am a poor excuse for one."

She was on her knees close to him in the healing water.

"Tell me about these bandits who killed your husband."

"My husband was panning in the mountains for gold. He had found some earlier, his partner told me. His compadre had come back home to check on things for both of us women. But when he went back he found Miguel had been murdered and robbed."

"Who was it?"

"They say it was Raul Gomez and his gang. I don't know him." Both of them were neck-deep in the swirling heated water. She shook her head as if she was disappointed. "I wish Gomez was dead."

"I agree. Did they say where this bandit lives?"

"Yes, south of St. Barnabas, on a big hacienda."

"How much gold do you think he had on him?"

"Oh, a few ounces maybe. But he was a very good prospector. I have a nice casa in my village we bought with gold he found up there. I think we would have had a good life together if they had not killed him."

"I can understand that. This man Gomez is a big bandit."

She shook her head. "He is a miserable bastard who preys on men like my Miguel. Gomez is a bully and someone needs to kill him."

He wiped his sweaty face with his hand and nodded. "Yes, someone needs to do that. I am ready to get out, and not to run you away."

She smiled openly. "Where would I run to?"

"Good, we can go to my camp." He stood up and started wading for the shore. She rose and the water droplets ran off her pear-shaped breasts. She gathered her clothes and walked to where he unfurled his bedroll, and they both sat down cross-legged. She put her clothes beside her, and he handed her a towel to dry herself with. In the afternoon heat the evaporation quickly cooled them after their hot water bath.

"Do you have a wife?" she asked, leaning back on her elbows.

"No wife. No house. You are at my place."

She openly laughed and shook her head, and that let her

shoulder-length hair fall back from her face. "Did any woman ever threaten to chain you up?"

"Hell, they'd turn me loose. Anyone tell you how many men this Gomez has?"

"They said he had an army. But I don't know. Why don't you have a wife?"

"I have enough problems taking care of myself."

"No, you have other secrets."

He agreed with her and went forward on his knees to kiss her. He made no attempt to hold her, but simply kissed her full bottom lip that looked so sweet. He thought she might have smeared some honey on her lips, and he moved into more contact with her sensuous body. Their movement toward each other proved to be like two perfectly machined gears coming perfectly in contact, and they rolled on.

Riding the waves of her body, Slocum built to a high crescendo, and when he finally came, they faded into a somber state of possessing each other.

He tasted her boobs. "You're an angel," he whispered in her ear.

"No, I can tell you make poor judgments. Angels do not fornicate."

"How do you know they don't?"

"The padre who once had sex with me as a teenager told me so."

They both laughed.

"Really?" he asked. "Did he really have sex with you?"

She wrinkled her nose to dismiss the matter. "Even in robes some men can be men."

"Tell me how I will find out all about this bastard Gomez?"

"I know a *puta* who lives over there who I grew up with. Go to her. I will give you a letter to her and she can tell you all about them."

"What will you do without your man to bring home gold?"

"Are you interested in a job and a wife?"

"I can't handle it."

"You did well this afternoon with me. You are a good seducer of women."

"Ah, but I must solve other things."

"Solve them and come back to my village and we will play house."

"I can think of few other women I'd rather do that with. I am concerned about your welfare."

"I am not as good as he was, but I can wash gold out of those iron filings."

"I salute you, lovely lady."

"Maybe we should do it another time."

He heard something. It was horses coming. "Get your clothes on and get out of sight. That may be trouble." He pulled on his pants and then put on his shirt. She was gone from sight when the riders halted close to his camp. They were tough-looking men.

"What're you doing here, gringo?" one of them demanded.

"I am no gringo, hombre, I am one of you."

Slocum wished that he had his gun in his hand. There were two of them. One was a big man and wore a knit stocking cap despite the heat. The shorter one dismounted holding a large, old Walker Colt cap-and-ball pistol in his hand and wearing a sombrero with a chin string tied down. He ordered, "Put your hands up, gringo. We want your gold."

"I have no gold, stupid. You have held up a poor man."

"We know this woman who was with you, and we know you have her gold."

"I have no gold. You're in the wrong place."

If only his own gun had been in his hand, he could have handled them. It was in the holster at the head of the bedroll on the ground.

"What are you doing here then?" the bigger one said, and his horse tried to twist around. The rider jerked on his bridle and the horse reared precariously high. Then in a flash Lupe appeared and whistled sharply. She tossed him the Spencer rifle. He cocked the hammer back, then fired at the shorter man on foot. The gun smoke from the .56/.52-caliber rimfire cartridge was blinding, and no wind stirred to remove it. The crazy horse had thrown the big man off.

Slocum set the rifle down and swept up his own handgun. He rushed over to see about the wounded short man on the ground.

"Who are you?" he demanded.

The short man held his right arm; he was obviously wounded in it, judging from the blood on his sleeve. Slocum picked up the Colt. He held the old revolver, which must have weighed nine pounds, in his left hand as he backed up to order the big man to get over there. He disarmed him of some old Civil War six-shooter. They sure had ancient armory on them.

"Find a rope, we'll tie them up," he said to Lupe.

She agreed and picked up the one tied on Slocum's saddle. Barefooted, she brought it over to him. He forced the two men to get on their bellies, and he tied their hands behind their backs.

Meanwhile she took their boots off and threw aside the knives that were concealed on them. She demanded, "Who are you *bastardos*?"

When they didn't answer her, she stomped on the short one's kidneys with her bare heel. "Damn it, tell me, and now."

"Oh, Mother of God, woman, my arm is killing me. My name is Santo Vantis. His name is Coffee Jack."

"Why Coffee Jack?" she demanded.

"I don't know. They always call him that."

"Did you know these men?" Slocum asked her.

"No. You, Santo, tell me how you know me."

"Don't kick me again. We heard you had gold your dead husband had gathered."

"Who told you?"

He shook his head. "I don't know his name."

"I think you must ride with that Gomez and you killed my husband."

"No, no."

"Don't lie to me. Tell me or you maybe be made into a gelding."

"We didn't kill him. Gomez killed him because he never would tell him where he hid his gold. We figured you knew where it was hidden and had gone up there and gotten it."

"Does Gomez know you came back up here?"

"No."

"What should we do with them?" She whirled to face Slocum, realizing then that there was a crowd of women who had come to see what had happened there.

She held her hand up to stop Slocum and turned to speak to the crowd. "Did you hear these bandits admit they killed my husband?"

Heads nodded. That was not enough for her. "What should we do with them? The Federales will only turn them loose."

"Hang them," one said, and the crowd quickly agreed.

"We will send for our men to come here and do that," another spoke up.

"No," a matron-like woman said. "We don't need our men. They killed her husband. We are not helpless. Catch their horses and bring them. I saw a strong-looking limb back there. They have ropes on their saddles. Get them, get them."

"You don't have to be in on this," Lupe said to Slocum.

"I am here." He had no use for the pair of admitted outlaws.

The mob of women who took charge of the two men were not gentle, and they kicked them in their butts to make them move forward. The swelling crowd moved up the road to the west. They had captured their horses as well.

Lupe had gone ahead to help them get the job dome.

Slocum wondered if she might know where her husband had hidden the gold. That was a new twist in her case. Obviously her man had been smart enough to hide the gold he'd panned, and she'd no doubt picked up a lead that might help her locate it. He hoped so. There was nothing he would do to save the two outlaws. They weren't worth saving, but the lack of law in this country also ensured there was no way to imprison them for any amount of time either.

He remained at the edge of the mob of angry women and wondered about the repercussions this lynching could flare up. Word of the hanging would soon spread, and vengeance would come hard on the outspoken ones—Lupe would be a chief suspect.

Ropes were tossed over tree limbs, and the men and their horses were brought into place. One woman with a strong voice gave a prayer. They all knelt and afterward made the sign of the cross on their fronts. The two crying men were put in their saddles, and two women hopped up behind them, one on each of their horses, to set the nooses over their heads. Then the executioners slid off the horses' butts. Both animals were handled at their bridles by two handlers apiece.

An older woman told the handlers to get aside, and they quickly did as she ordered. Then she sliced the air with her arm like an axe and the women behind beat the horses' butts. They spooked away and the two men danced on the ropes. The big man did little of that; his neck must have been broken. The short one strangled, but soon he was still.

All the women were on their knees praying for them, and some were counting rosary beads. The older woman came over.

"Now, señor, what must we do?"

"Cut them down. Burn the nooses in a hot fire, bury them and their saddles in a deep hole. I would take the horses a great distance away from here, cut their throats, and remove their brands. Leave them for the buzzards to eat. Then swear everyone to secrecy. Someone will talk, but what can they find?"

She nodded in agreement. "I appreciate your information. We will do that then go home."

"If they come for revenge, you must band together as you did today. Her husband's killers are gone. That is good, but there will be some demand for more blood for this last act."

"I savvy."

He turned on his heel and started back for his camp. Lupe stopped him. Her eyes were red from crying. In a low voice she said she must help them carry out his instructions. "I will see you in camp."

"I will be there."

"I think I know where his gold is hidden now." She looked at him very seriously.

"That's good."

She stood up on her toes and kissed him on the mouth. "I owe you much."

He shook his head, but by then she'd hurried off to help the others.

That night, after they ate some beans for supper, they went to bed together, and she clung to him all night. Twice he awoke and she was whimpering over her loss. He hugged her tightly and she soon slept again. Before dawn, in the canyon's coolest hour, they slipped off naked hand in hand to soak in the hot water.

Neck-deep in the water that was steaming clouds of fog, he asked where she thought the gold might be.

"There is a shrine beside the trail, for a woman and her family who were killed by a band of Apaches on that mountain. I think he may have hid it there. It is a very well-made shrine built by stone craftsmen, and while her name is lost, he called it Mary's Shrine."

"That may be the place. Good luck. I must go on my way today."

"I understand, but I live east of here, in the Valley of Fire. Come by and see me if you can. The *puta* I know at St. Barnabas is Carla Miquey. Tell her Lupe sent you."

"I will do that."

They kissed, and he departed after breakfast. He was going west again, over the mountain, to reach the road that went south. The hot springs treatment had helped ease his back muscles, but Lupe was still on his mind.

But he rode on—he had promised Dan he'd check out this Gomez's outfit and its strength.

4

The trip to St. Barnabas took two days, and he stopped at many cantinas, sat with his back to the wall, drank straight mescal, and talked to *putas* who wanted to take him to bed. Instead he fed them and himself and learned all they knew about this outlaw Gomez.

At last, he arrived in what would prove to be the village closest to their hideout. He stabled his horse and took a room in a whorehouse. Business was slow, and the madam told him that for his twenty-five cents he could sleep there but got no free pussy. He went to the busiest cantina, took a place in the shadows, and ordered food and mescal. Soon a young *puta* was there like a buzzard at a cow killing.

"You are lonely back here?" she asked.

He saw her as a skinny dumb girl in his first gaze at her. She scooted close to him and sniffed the fumes coming off his plate of meat, sweet peppers, and onions—and hot ones too.

He handed her a flour tortilla, and she got on her knees

on the bench to load it for him from the sizzling pan. Leaned back, he waited for her to get the tortilla wrapped. When she'd completed the task, she fed it to him.

"You like me?" She smiled big at him.

"You will do."

"Oh, but hombre, I can care for you. You like this no?"

"What do they call you?"

"Roma."

"Roma, huh?"

"*Sí*. I would make you a wonderful companion."

"Where would you go?"

"Anywhere you like. I could comfort you at night and in the day care for you."

"What if I don't need a woman?"

"Oh, I bet when I get through feeding you, you will need one bad."

"Is there a woman working here named Carla Miquey?"

"No, she went to Porta Dia-yamia with a man who liked her. You know her?"

"No, but a friend of mine said she thought she was here and could help me. Do you know any of Gomez's men?"

She curled her lip. "They are dumb *bastardos*. I hate when they come to town. Are you going to join them?"

He shook his head and took another bite from her wrap. By this time, she had moved to sit astraddle of his lap. When she moved over, she hiked her dress above her butt, and her bare legs surrounded him. It wasn't hard to tell she had no underwear on. But why wear any? She'd just have to take it off for the next guy. She held his tortilla in both hands for him to eat it.

She wrinkled her nose at him. "They are dumb too."

"How dumb?"

"They make big robberies, but his men do not get paid.

He pays them like peons, not soldiers like he needs. You would not talk to them, they are so dumb."

"But they make big raids."

"Ah, like an army they have a *generale* and he leads them to their slaughter, no?"

"So all the power is in his hands, huh?"

She gave him another bite. "More or less, huh?"

"Yes, of course. Where is this army headquartered at?"

"Oh, he has a hacienda south of here. It once was a grand place when I was a little girl. Now it is a dried-up turd."

"Dried-up turd?"

"Yes, he didn't irrigate the grapes and the citrus, and it all died of course."

"So he doesn't farm any longer?"

"No."

"How many men are out there?"

"Maybe two dozen, laying around sleeping all day, and they have some old hags out there and he buys them cheap wine."

"Oh, I thought he had an army."

She dismissed his concern with a head shake.

He finished his meal and took her to his room in the whorehouse.

"Why do you live here?" she demanded in the street, realizing where he was taking her.

"It is cheap."

"How cheap?"

"Twenty-five cents a day."

"Cheap enough." She raised her skirt hem and crossed the ditch to sashay up the steps ahead of him.

What a yickity-yack he had found this time. Maybe she knew more about Gomez. He would find out. And then perhaps she'd shut up. He hoped that he'd finally get Roma to stop talking. They went in his room and he closed the door. She undressed herself and then began to undress him. He hung up his gun belt on a ladder-back chair.

"That is a pretty holster." She bent over to look at it. "I like it. You want me in the bed?"

"No. I don't need your body. I need your brain."

"No, no, you are being sweet to me. I can handle that." She hugged him, and the top of her head did not come to his chin. She kissed her chest and swirled the hair with her tongue.

He held her out at his arm's length. "Stop. I don't want your body. I have to find out about this outlaw Gomez."

"People don't expect much from crazy people, do they?"

He let her go now that that was settled.

"No, they sure don't. I can't understand you about half the time," he said, amused at her, and him seated on the chair to remove his spurs so she could slip off his boots.

"I am going to sleep. You can sleep here if you want to. But you must stop talking. In the morning I am going to check on this outlaw. I don't need a wife or a lover tonight."

"Why did you bring me here then?"

"'Cause I could not get rid of you."

"You have a brush? I need to brush my hair."

His britches on, he bent over and threw her one from his war bag. She went to work brushing her hair hard, and it began to become more manageable. "You got a wife?"

"No."

"You got a house?"

"No."

"No wonder you don't have a wife. No house."

"Who needs a house?"

"For a wife to keep the kids dry inside it."

"I don't have any kids. How hard would it be to look over Gomez's place?"

"I'd probably have to screw a guard. While you looked inside it, huh?"

"Did I say that?"

"No, but you thought it. Here's your brush back. It is a nice one."

"You know where I keep it now."

"Don't me sitting around here naked make you horny?"

"Roma, it does not, and I need to see the inside of his fort tonight."

She gave him an impatient head toss. "Get dressed and we will get that over with *tonight*."

"You certain we can get in there and, more important, get out and not get caught?"

"I can distract them and you can slip inside."

"I would not ask that of you."

"So what? He won't be the last or the first one to screw me, huh?"

"All right, but I'll make it up with you. Get dressed—"

"Aw hell. Well, next time." She pouted.

Slocum and Roma, dressed for a long ride, went out, and rode double for Gomez's operation.

The sun was setting fast as they approached the place. She said for Slocum to head for the southwest and they would have some cover, rather then ride across the barren fields and bare vineyard. She pointed the way as the moon began to rise. When they were within a half mile of the dark buildings, they left his horse and went on foot. He had the Spencer rifle, just in case, and wore both bandoliers.

"I will distract the guard and make him go with me behind a wall, so you can slip inside. Be careful—they may not be asleep in there. I can keep him there until you get out. Toss a small pebble over the wall, and I will tell him it was just a bat and leave him. You will wait at the horse for me? I don't come in a while, you go on. I can screw my way out of there."

They waited until around midnight, then she went ahead and soon struck up a soft conversation with a guard. At last Slocum heard her ask him, "You want some pussy?"

"Sure."

"Let's go behind the wall and no one will see us."

"Sure."

Slocum waited and then watched the guard following her. This was his chance. They had no platforms set up on the walls to shoot off. That was good. They couldn't be up there taking potshots at any attackers. He saw their ammo and guns inside the front door, right adjacent to the entrance. A well-placed arrow shot over that wall with a stick of blasting powder would cause a hell of an explosion. Good he had that down.

In the yard with only a low wall around it was the well. They could be held away from water by just about anyone, unless they crawled out there and no one outside the yard could see them. But they still had to rise up to get the water out—they could be shot then. Bars were on most of the side windows.

Slocum decided he'd seen enough to raid the place and strike hard enough to knock them out. Back inside, he could hear lots of snoring. He came out of the house in a crouching run, threw a small rock over the wall, and beat it outside to some cover.

From cover, he saw Roma and the guard returning in the silver light to his post. He was buttoning his pants and talking to her. He bent over and kissed her, felt her ass, and she left him laughing. She skipped by where Slocum crouched and said softly, "It went fine."

He watched for anyone trailing her. None came. Then he got up and went to their horse.

"You see it all?" she asked.

"Yes. We can take it. That is what I wanted to see."

"Now let's go up to this place that is a hideout way back in the tules. There is a cabin up there. Feed for your horse and enough to eat. Nothing fancy."

"Where is that?"

"I can get you there in the morning."

"Who owns it?"

"A man I know. I can use it."

"All right, you deserve my attention for a day or two after all you've done."

Riding behind him, she hit him on the right shoulder with her fist. "Let's go to the cabin in the morning."

"I'll be ready."

They rode out of St. Barnabas before the sun rose and climbed into the mountains on a dim road. Midday they were in the pines, and the air was full of resins and cooler air. With Roma on the back of his cantle and hugging him, the pacing horse made good time getting up there. She pointed Slocum, to a side trail and he took that lead. In a short while, he spotted the small cabin in a grassy meadow where there was also obviously a spring, for there were tules.

"Who owns this?" he asked.

"A man I know. We can use it. It has food and supplies and I have a key to it."

"This sure looks handy."

"I have stayed up here before. It is a good place and no one will bother us here."

"I will keep my guard up. The last place I was at was a women's hot springs. I even delivered a baby there, or the women thought I did. But two of Gomez's men came to kill me and also a woman I met there."

"Who were they?"

"One was Santo Vantis, and the other Jack somebody."

"Coffee Jack was his name. He was a big goon that worked for Gomez."

Slocum leaned over. "They are both playing harps somewhere now."

She giggled. "No, those two are stoking the fires of hell."

She made them flour tortillas and wrapped them around some beans she'd cooked. He hobbled the horse, who was harvesting the grass, and got back in time to eat. She sat on his lap, with her dress hiked over her slender ass, and fed him.

"This is like a dream for me. I don't have to go find customers, and we can leisurely do what we want to do for a few days, huh?" She wiggled her butt on his legs.

"Two days and I need to go back to Arizona."

"Oh. Make it three, or even stay a week." She kissed him on the mouth.

"Wish I could. But I promised some people I'd get back."

"Oh, well," she sighed. "Then I better get busy so you won't want to leave me."

It was the middle of the night and Slocum woke up in some kind of hell. A flurry of boots were kicking the hell out of him. Roma was fighting like a wildcat and screaming. It was dark as pitch in the cabin, and the attackers were cussing, stinky sweaty ones.

He managed to get up. Then he was tossed aside by a hunk of a man and fell on top of his own Bowie knife, which luckily was flat on the floor. His finger closed on the handle, and his next move was to roll over and slash the attacker's leg. The razor-sharp edge went clear to the man's shinbone, and the victim screamed like a wounded bear. Another man reached for Slocum, and the Bowie blade cut open his lower arm. The attackers were leaving out the door, but he stabbed another in the back before he reached it who gasped and went down. Slocum fell over him, and then he went back for his rifle. In the moonlight he could see the others getting on their horses to flee.

And he took aim. The rifle bucked hard into his shoulder with each shot. The boiling gunpowder smoke burned his eyes. He fired the seven rounds, quickly laying down men and horses. Then he rushed inside, found another tube, and jammed it in the butt.

"Oh, be careful," Roma said after him.

She was hurt, he knew, but finishing off these raiders was more important for the moment. He hoped her injuries were not serious, as he levered a new round into the chamber and crossed the moonlit meadow. Men lay moaning on the ground all around him. When they tried to rise up to shoot him, he shot them, until they all were dead or at least silent. Then he shot their wounded horses.

He jerked up by his hair one of the attackers who was begging for his life—the last one alive. "Who in the damn hell sent you here?"

"Colonel Gomez."

He looked down. The man was holding his blood-darkened shirt in both hands. "You're gut-shot, mister. You'd better go to praying that God's coming for you."

He went back to the house, and Roma staggered out the door. Her face was dark in blood, and she was holding the right side under her palm.

"What's the matter?"

"That big bastard gouged out my eye."

"Good God, girl. Which one of them was it?"

"The one you cut his leg artery and he's bleeding to death, but my eye socket hurts real bad."

He set down the rifle and hugged her. "I'm so sorry. I never expected they'd find us up here. We need to get you to a doctor. Is the closest one in St. Barnabas?"

"Yes. What will I do?"

"He can't put it back. But he can stop the bleeding and numb it."

She squeezed him harder. "What will I do? A one-eyed whore? Oh, Slocum, why did he do that to me?"

He looked off at the mountain silhouettes. Just a mean son of a bitch was all he could think.

"I want you to sit down. I don't care if the buzzards and wolves eat them, but I am going to drag the bodies out of the house so they don't rot and ruin your friend's nice cabin, then we will ride for the doctor."

"Oh, Slocum, who were they?"

"The guy dying over there said Gomez's."

"He'll pay for this. Go ahead."

He dragged two bodies out and left them a few yards from the house. But it required a rope around his legs and a horse on the end to pull the biggest dead man's body outside and away from the house.

In the cabinets Slocum found a bottle of laudanum and took it out to Roma with a spoon.

"Take one tablespoon. I need to go saddle my horse. We will bandage your head up and then ride for town."

She agreed. The blood flow looked to be less, but he knew she was in great pain. At last his own horse was saddled, bedroll tied on, the Spencer reloaded and in his scabbard. He found some crackers and filled a couple of canteens with water from the spring. Then he did the best he could with bandages and gauze to wrap that side of her face.

"Has it let up some?" he asked her.

She nodded.

Laudanum bottle and spoon in his saddlebags, he left the dead bandits for the buzzards. They'd soon be there, with the dawn coming.

He picked her up, and holding her in his arms, he stepped aboard and they left the mountain cabin for St. Barnabas.

Twice he fed her more medicine, and she remained in a groggy stage the entire trip, which took the better part of the day. They'd both eaten a few crackers and drank some canteen water.

His arms ached from holding her all the way, but he delivered her to the doctor's door, having been guided to his house by an old woman's directions. A woman opened the doctor's front door, and behind her bustling skirt, she ushered Slocum in and to a lighted room.

"What's happened to her?"

"Some thug gouged out her eye."

"Oh my, that is horrible. He's . . . ?"

"Dead. I have given her pain medicine. She's had little to eat all day. It took us all day to get here from the mountains where it happened. She is very brave."

"Doctor, she lost her eye last night," she said to the graying man who came into the room, putting the glasses on the end of his nose.

"I can't reattached it," he said to Slocum.

"I know that. I want you to save her life."

"I will try. But so you know."

"I didn't expect it, but she deserves to live."

The doctor took scissors from the woman and began to remove the bandages. "You may go get something to eat. I will have to tie off blood veins and clear the area involved."

"I'll be back, she has no one."

When Slocum walked out, a gentleman dismounted and approached him. "My name is Martin Wade. I was informed you just brought in a young woman of interest to me who was injured."

"Roma?"

"Yes."

"Do you have a cabin in the mountains?"

The man nodded.

"A very nice place. Folks call me Slocum," Slocum said and extended his hand, which Wade shook. "A half dozen of Gomez's men caught us sleeping and attacked us. One of them gouged out her right eye in the fight. He's dead, and so are the rest. None are inside the cabin, but I left them for the buzzards in the yard, and their dead horses too."

Wade blinked blinked his eyes in disbelief. "A wonder you two survived."

Slocum agreed. "My guard was down up there. Obviously we were followed. They snuck up in the night and began kicking and beating us. We had the fight of our lives, I can assure you, but I never expected that thug to hurt her like that. He literally spooned out her eyeball with his thumb. But he's dead, and he bled to death getting there."

"Good riddance. I will pay for her medical care. I'll send some of my men up there and clean up the mess. Thanks for protecting her."

"Sorry, we both were planning a rest up there for a few days. It was a wonderful place, sorry it was used by them as an attack point."

"How is she?" Wade made a head toss at the lighted doorway.

"A strong person. She should survive."

"My wife died a few years ago. Roma is a very free spirit. I enjoy her company."

"I can understand that."

"Where will you eat?"

"I had not decided."

"Come to my casa. My cook will feed you and you can

rest there. Let me speak to Dr. Mendoza and then we can go up there."

"I'll put up my horse—"

"No, I have a stable. He can be there."

Wade hurried inside and then came out. They walked three blocks to his walled casa, leading Slocum's mount. The place was obviously guarded by the armed man on the wall who gave Wade a salute in the night. He returned it.

A stableman took Slocum's horse. Wade showed him the front doorway that was open.

A very efficient-looking lady greeted them.

"Zelda, this is Slocum. I fear he's not eaten in a long time. Can we scare him up some food and perhaps some good whiskey to sip on while it is being fixed?"

"I think there is slight breeze on the patio upstairs. Retire to there and the rest will be attended to. Nice to meet you, sir." She slightly curtsied to him.

"Zelda, my name is Slocum. No big deal."

"I will remember that—Slocum." She nodded, as if excused, and went to the rear.

Wade showed him the stairs, and they went up to sit out under the stars.

"I can see you have been in many tight situations in your life. This near-death event has not shaken you?"

Slocum shook his head. "I consider it really a small event by some stupid goons, who could have taken command of the situation, then beat the hell out of us under pointed guns."

"What is your purpose down here?"

"I came to see how big and how smart this Gomez is. His border raids have not made him liked up there. Do you think he is being left alone because the Federales fear him?"

"Good question. I have no idea, but so far they have ridden around him."

"Is he paying them off?"

"That would be hard to learn."

"He looks to be immune to them controlling him despite his actions to run over people, to murder, rape, and rob them."

Wade agreed, and Zelda served them whiskey in crystal tumblers with a bottle standing by.

Slocum raised his glass to his host. "Thanks."

Damn good whiskey. The liquor slid down his throat and washed away a ton of trail dust. Slocum breathed easier— real damn good booze.

"I am curious," Wade began. "A man and a gun came here like David with Goliath?"

"I didn't come to kill him. I came to look at his strength and weaknesses, to see if his activity here and north of the border could be shut down. He's made some raids to rustle cattle across that line. Along with rape, pillage, and the death of a small boy. He needs to be stopped. But the people up there want him permanently stopped."

His hostess delivered him his hot food, and he thanked her.

"Go ahead and eat," Wade said.

Slocum cut up some of the braised beef, and his first forkful drew saliva in his mouth. Excellent beef mesquite-roasted was hard to beat. He swept up some red mashed beans with a fresh flour tortilla. Wade let him eat.

"He has a strong fortress down there."

"An Achilles' heel too. They all have them. I think he can be stopped. What would you like to do?"

"There are several businesspeople in the region who would like to see him gone as well."

"Good. Can they be considered honest?"

"How is that?"

"Can you promise me they won't run and tell him our plans?"

"I think so."

"I can't afford him being warned."

"What else?"

"Would they send armed men to help us?"

"Some would."

"Line me up to talk to only the most trustworthy."

Wade poured them more whiskey. "I will choose them after a thorough investigation."

"Good. I will be back to see you after I talk to my people and they decide how they want to handle this matter."

"Get some sleep. I will send one of my girls that works for us down to the doctor's, and she can report to us if there is any change in Roma's condition. I appreciate you rescuing her. She's a darling."

"Good."

"What else do you need?"

"A few hours' shut-eye and I'll be fine. Thanks for the food and the whiskey. I need to go back north. Tomorrow, I need to start that way, after I check on Roma, but I appreciate you caring for her."

"Could I send a few men with you?"

Slocum shook his head. "That would only draw attention to me and make them more wary."

"Good enough. But come here if you need asylum."

Slocum cracked a smile. "That could be a lifesaver at times, thanks, my *amigo*."

Roma was still in a state of shock when he squeezed her hand and was ready to leave her. "Wade will see you recover. I spoke with him. I must get back, as you know. God bless you, girl. You are a sweet woman."

She slightly shook her head on the pillow. "May God be with you too, big hombre."

In the coolness of the dawn, he set out on the pacing horse, headed northward through the tall cactus that differed from the Arizona saguaros. Why did he feel followed? Had more of the outlaw chief's men found him? No way to see them, even if they were right behind him in the tall vegetation. He set the horse in a grinding pace to force anyone following to come into the open and make more dust on his back trail.

When he came to a rise, he crossed over it. Then once he was over the top, he reined up the horse. Dismounted, he took out the Spencer and went back to peek over the ridge without his hat on.

Three tough riders were indeed following his trail and hurrying their horses in a flurry of dust. Since he couldn't be too sure of their identity, he decided to take out their horses and leave them a hell of a walk back.

He took aim and shot the horse to the right of him. The wreck spilled the horse's rider off over its head and nosed the animal down into a death dive. The others reined up. Even in the dust and distance Slocum saw the shock written on their faces. He shot the next rider's horse, and it reared and fell over backward.

Number three tried to turn his horse around and run for cover. But two quickly placed shots from the Spencer and the man's horse spilled over. Even at the space between them he could hear them cursing him.

"*Vaya con Dios, hombres*," he said quietly, then put on his hat and rode for the border.

There were no more incidents with Gomez's men. But he learned in Nogales that the Apaches were still raiding the area. Some Mexican Apache chief named Who had caught a company of cavalry unaware and slaughtered them up near the Whetstone Mountains, west of Tombstone. The army really was pouring in lots more troops according to reports.

But as the Mexican man at the border said, "Who can catch the wind?"

He rode into Patagonia with light rain falling on his hat and shoulders. This was a rare treat. Thunder rumbled off in the mountains to the south. His horse put up at the stables, he walked the two blocks to the hotel and discovered Sandy in the lobby reading a newspaper.

She blinked at his entrance and then smiled. She must have forgotten for a second that she had seen him in his border garb.

She folded the newspaper and rose, very proper. "I wondered how you were."

Hat in hand, he admired her. Too many people were there in the lobby for him to kiss her, so he winked at her instead. "I'd have thought they'd have it settled it by now."

She turned up her hands. "It has really gotten worse."

"I saw where the company of soldiers were ambushed. I need a bath, but that can wait. Let's go find a meal."

"Surely. You will have to tell me all about Mexico and what you found out down there."

"Tortillas, frijoles, and hot peppers," he went on, until she elbowed him and shook her head.

The café was busy, but they found a table.

"Have you been occupied?" he asked, seating her and then sitting himself down across from her. His hat stowed under his chair, he told her to continue.

"I was upset when you left, but I understood you needed to be alone to do that job. Our trip over here was so nail-biting scary, and I am certain down there was no better, but there was some kind of challenge in me that I wished I'd gone along."

"I may have to return down there. But they won't leave the ranch unattended with all those war parties around. So we may have some time together if you can spare it."

"Spare it? I'd love to have some more time in your company."

"I would too." He winked at her. "The like might ruin your reputation."

She looked down, putting the cloth napkin in her lap. "I could do a lot of that too."

They both laughed softly. A tinge of blush in her cheeks, and she shook her head to dismiss her remark. What a lovely lady. Considering Slocum's own wild past with shady ladies, she was such an outstanding individual to have in his life, living in the protective custody of this village before she returned to her rural schoolhouse to teach young people how to read, write, and become grown-ups in a bloody world. Many of them had learned about this deadly knife's edge of frontier at their own homes in these raids.

"Did you settle anything down there?"

"Gomez is a powerful force. But like these Apaches, he is controllable."

She nodded. They ordered their meal and talked about her meeting some people and how her parents in Kansas were well and they had gotten her letter saying that she'd arrived.

"The mail does continue to come through," she said.

"Yes. But I am surprised there aren't more troops down here to protect the country."

"How will they get here?" she asked. "There is no train coming through on unseen tracks."

He agreed. The lady understood many deeply thought things about the world they lived in. What a delightful companion he had to share a meal with, besides her beauty that turned men's heads. And she was his to savor. My, how this event beat spying on old outlaws below the border.

"After lunch, if I have to bathe in the creek, I am getting a bath." He shook his head over his soggy condition.

"It has stopped raining."

"Good."

"What are your plans?"

Under his breath he said, "Get a bath and entertain you in your room tonight."

"Oh," she said softly. "That would be wonderful."

He reached over and squeezed her hand. "It will be."

The meal arrived, and they ate the hot food and washed it down with strong coffee. Then he walked her back to the hotel and left to find a bath.

There was no bathhouse open in town. The Chinaman who had run one had left for parts unknown. Slocum took a towel from the hotel, and on the way bought a new shirt and pants that he found in a mercantile store. He went to the creek and located an isolated spot to wade in and wash his body and hair. Dressed under the cottonwoods, he slung his gun belt over his shoulder and headed back to find a barber. There was one waiting for him in his chair when he walked up the busy street and found him.

"Nice day," the man said, swinging a sheet over Slocum.

He soon had his haircut and his face closely shaved, while hearing all the gossip about the military's action or lack of it. And the story about the woman who ran off on her husband with another man, leaving him five children to raise by himself. And how she should have been driven back to her duty with a buggy whip popping her on the ass the whole trip back.

Slocum paid the barber, still amused at his solution to the desertion case. It was suppertime and he went to take Sandy out to eat. The streets were full of children playing and shouting. Wagons loaded with household goods parked all over town waiting to return to their places. The facilities of the town were badly stressed.

Diseases would soon fester in this sore spot if no one moved. Slocum might need to move Sandy to a better place. Tucson was no place to take her. Dead animals rotted on the street there. Wastewater puddled in the same place. Tombstone was a sin palace full of whores and their consorts—he didn't have many options.

She met him in the hotel lobby, and they returned to the same café. She mentioned that she felt it was the best place in town, though like the others it ran out of simple things.

The waiter told them they had fresh beef but no potatoes, and he could offer them rice or brown beans instead. "I am so sorry, but getting produce here is extremely hard, and Tombstone has the money to outbid us."

Slocum agreed, and they ordered rice with gravy.

"It is so good to have you here."

"Good to be here and only hid out from the Apaches and not bandits."

"I would love to see Mexico."

"It is a different land. The ordinary people down there are delightful. The outlaws have sharp teeth."

She nodded. "You have seen lots of that?"

"Too much. I wish I had a Garden of Eden I could move you to where you'd be safer."

"Why? I am managing here."

"This town is overloaded. A simple disease takes hold here, and it will become a wildfire under the current conditions."

She nodded thoughtfully. "Where could I go?"

"And be safe? I don't know, or we'd be on our way there."

She agreed, and they finished their meal. In the bleeding sunset, they went back to her room at the hotel. Finally behind the closed door, they were clinched in each other's arms and kissing, hungry for more and more.

"I had to come back," he whispered and kissed her harder.

"Why didn't we meet in Kansas and run off to live in this place you suggested? I would never have had to bury him and cry a widow's tears. To have traveled by stage to Bowie and us then to be thrown together in the midst of this Apache uprising, to have the sweet moments of the personal life we have shared . . . I thanked God for those events. I don't care if we break the law of Moses. Here in your arms is heaven to me, heaven on earth. A song I never found even with him. We made love, but it was simple and very mechanical. You are a thunderstorm and I hear it approaching us."

They sat in a chair, dressed and holding each other. Only the reasoning blasting in his brain, saying over and over again, *You can't keep her.*

5

He rode the next day out to Dan Delight's ranch and found him and his hands fortified like an army fort, with wagons overturned and barriers set up all around to deflect a direct horseback raid.

Slocum frowned at all the reinforcements at the ranch.

"They ambushed an army patrol," Dan said

"But have they even ridden by here?"

"No, but we're ready. What did you learn in Mexico? Come in the house."

"I learned that with a handful of men we can take on his fortress and close them down."

"We can't do it right now and leave the ranch vulnerable." He poured some whiskey into separate tin cups on the table.

"I understand. If you could hire me six tough men, I'd go do it and end his reign over those people and his raids up here. He sent some men after me, and I owe him an eye for the eye they gouged out of a poor girl who was with me down there."

Dan frowned. "Who was she?"

"A young woman who distracted a guard while I found all the arms Gomez has for the defense of the hacienda. We were later attacked and she lost her eye. She is in good care now, but she won't ever get her vision back."

"You can still get women to help you do anything." Dan shook his head in disbelief. "I can't leave here with them out there. I damn sure want him knocked out of business, but I can't go right now."

"Even a powerful Mexican can figure out why I looked at his fort, and it will be tighter and harder to get inside."

"Slocum, all I have is this ranch. That bastard Gomez not only stole my cattle, but he has hurt many people in Mexico flexing his power. He and his men killed a man whom I considered my adopted brother, Alfredo Morales, and sold his wife into slavery as a whore. She was killed before I could have her rescued. He has raped innocent children and then he also sold many more in the white slave trade."

"He needs to be removed."

"Oh yes, he does," Dan said. "Tell me, they say the Apaches stole the gold at that mine they struck?"

"They got a good lesson on what gold could buy for them—guns, ammunition, food and other goods, horses—hell, they know the whole system now. They rob a stage, they get the money and gold in the strongboxes."

"I'll be damned. All these years I thought they were ignorant."

"They aren't. Give me three tough men and I'll find the others and get this Gomez. If you want him wiped off the map, we need to do it now."

"That would leave us awfully short of guns to defend this ranch. They finished off an army patrol up by the Whetstones."

"That army patrol were probably foreigners and they rode

into a trap. They have not gone against anything barricaded like this place."

"Hell, I'll get you two. Where will you get the rest?"

"I'll have to hire them—somewhere."

Dan brought him two men, Ken Highland, a Texan who Slocum decided probably was on the run from the law. Tall, thick-set, with blue eyes. Judging by the way he wore a gun, he'd make a good hand. He spit tobacco aside and in a rusty voice said, "We going down there for a party?"

"Damn right, and when we get the place flattened, we will celebrate Mexican style."

"Good enough. I heard enough about you. I'll foller you."

"Thanks."

Jewels Cline was a bucktoothed kid. Skinny as a rail and maybe eighteen. His too-long blond hair was like straw sticking out from under his hatband. He had only fuzz on his cheeks and a lazy right eye.

"You see all right?" Slocum asked.

He smiled. "I can see. You want to see me shoot for you?"

"Sure," Slocum said. "One of you guys set up some bottles down there against that hill. That suit you?"

"Fuck yes."

The Kid swaggered around until the bottles were set up. Then he nodded with a smug set to his lips, drew his pistol, and rapid-fired five rounds—four struck brown glass; the other one was close, spitting dust beside the empty bottle.

"Good enough," Slocum said. The boy could sure hit what he aimed at.

Slocum made certain each man had two pistols and a working rifle with ammo. He told them he would meet them in three days near the Willows. But they were not to go into the saloon/whorehouse on the Mexican border, deep in a canyon with some water seeps so that willows flourished.

Dan was supplying Slocum with three packhorses and the food they'd need for two weeks. He told Dan's two men that he would find them at the Willows and take them to a safe haven. No one else needed to know anything about their business there.

Slocum left them that night and rode back to Patagonia. When Sandy descended out the hotel front door, he met her and they went to breakfast. The squatters and their wagons were still parked all over in the crowded streets.

"How has it gone so far?"

"I have half an army, but I need to hire two or three more specialists I know."

"Specialists?" She held the coffee cup at her mouth waiting for his answer.

"I need someone who can shoot a bow and arrow."

"Where is he?"

"No doubt sobering up in a wickiup over by the fort."

"Who else?" She smiled at him.

"A big burly Mexican named Gordon who farms among the Mormons up at St. David."

"Will they come help you?"

"For a fee they would do anything."

"I see. How long will you be gone this time?"

"Not over two weeks I hope."

"Things are calming down. I may have to go back to my schoolhouse or lose my job."

"You need any money?"

She put her hands out in protest. "I will be fine. If I am not here, then you will know where I will be."

"That's fine. I can find you. If you go back, be careful. All this Apache warfare may not be over."

"I understand. Will you sleep a few hours in my room?"

"A few. I need to get over to the fort and find my man."

Back in the room she helped him undress. "Should I wake you?"

"By three o'clock."

She nodded, putting aside his clothing. "I will wake you by then."

Last sight he had of her was sitting up proper in a chair and reading a leather-bound book. He needed no rocking to go to sleep. In late afternoon she awoke him.

He dressed, and she turned her back until he cleared his throat.

"Every time you leave me, I almost cry. Then you come back and I am elated."

"Sorry, but I need to close this business in Mexico while I can. He's vulnerable now—but he could get better reinforced and it would take an army to shake him."

"Ride careful. I will pray for you."

"Thanks." He kissed her and then left.

In an hour Slocum was back in the saddle and headed for Fort Huachuca. There was breed who was settled near the fort and lived with a Mexican wife.

He found them at sundown. And with a warm smile Charlie Horse invited him to get down. They went and squatted under a small mesquite tree.

"I need someone who can shoot arrows."

"I know one." He grinned.

"This is in Mexico."

He made a solemn nod. "When?"

"Meet me at the Willows in two days. There are two men from Dan's ranch going to be there waiting. A bucktoothed kid, and a big Texan, Ken Highland, is in charge."

"Who else will you take along?"

"Gordon."

"He's tough enough. I will be there."

"Does your wife need some money?" Slocum drew out ten dollars and handed it to him for her.

"Thanks, *amigo*. That will do her. I will meet you at Willows."

After hugging Charlie's wife, Slocum left there and in the growing darkness rode on north through the desert to St. David. Under the moonlight, he crossed the muddy-bottomed San Pedro River and got down his bedroll to sleep until dawn.

He woke before daybreak, put up his bedroll, and rode the pacing horse up the lane to an adobe jacal. A huge man stood in the doorway and frowned, then swept the dark hair from his face. "Where were you last night?"

"Sleeping down by the river, why?"

"Why didn't you come up here?"

"Didn't want to bother you or Alma."

Shorter than him by over a foot, his wife ducked her head past the man in the doorway. "That would not have bothered us. Get in here and eat."

"I am coming." Amused, Slocum hitched his horse and came through the yard gate.

"What are you doing about these Apaches running around?"

"Avoiding them." He hugged her tight.

"Where have you been?" she asked, guiding him inside.

"Oh, around."

"Around wild women I bet. Sit down. We have lots of food or I'll make more."

"I never saw when you didn't have enough. How are the Mormon and Catholic getting along?"

She shook her head. "Just fine."

"She says that, but she wants me to take on more wives."

Her threatening finger in Gordon's face drew a big laugh from both men. They settled in and ate breakfast.

"You must need help," she said, passing the biscuits again to Slocum.

"I have a deal needs attention."

"Oh, needs attention." She took back the platter.

"There is a bandit down in Mexico needs removing. Everyone up here is watching for Apaches who they can't find. I want Gordon to go south with me for a week or so and help me straighten this matter out."

She nodded and said to her husband, "I can do the irrigation this week."

"Good. I am meeting the others tomorrow at the Willows."

"I can be there," Gordon said.

"What will you do now?" Alma asked Slocum.

"Oh, I'm going back to Patagonia and see about a friend, then I'll head for the Willows."

"Are there lots of folks staying at Patagonia?"

"Yes. The Apaches have been prowling around there. They struck a mine or two earlier. They attacked the two of us before we reached there over a week ago. But no one has seen them since the attack on the army patrol. You know they are like the wind."

"There are several folks from around here who live out on scattered ranches, who are staying here in town until all is clear. They are the most vulnerable."

He agreed and finished his coffee, then rose to his feet. "You make great coffee for a person doesn't drink it," he told Alma.

They all three laughed.

He rode back to Patagonia and joined Sandy in the hotel in mid-afternoon. She hugged him hard inside the room. "How are things going?"

"Good. I have my strike force assembled, and in a week we should be through."

"I received a letter from the school board. They said I should stay here until all reports of Apaches show they are gone or that they are subdued."

"Good." He moved her shoulder-length hair back and kissed her again. With her hands around his neck, she clung to him.

"You look so tired today. Will you rest some here?"

"I can do that. Thanks. I will be all right."

He sprawled on top of her bed and she read a book while he slept.

After his long nap they went for supper at sundown. Long shadows were cast down the street, and the children quieted from their playing. One donkey brayed loudly to another. The restaurant was crowded, but they found a table.

The waiter took their order and they sipped on hot coffee.

"When will this be all over?"

Slocum shook his head. "I have no idea, but with this many soldiers in the field it should end soon."

She nodded, then their food was there.

The food was good, considering the problems the merchants had securing enough via the freight wagons, which had been stalled by the Apache activity but were now guarded by the black soldier patrols to get them through to the overfilled town from Tucson and the east.

After the meal, he kissed her lightly on the boardwalk and went for his pacing horse. It was a few hours' ride to the Willows, and he wanted to meet the others quietly there.

His plans were slowly forming how he must divide his force and then bring them together again outside the Gomez hacienda. It needed to be carefully arranged not to draw attention. But Gomez only knew him, so perhaps that would work all right.

6

Well off the road to the Willows, he rode up to a lone jacal with a garden off the dim wagon tracks, on the creek north of his planned meeting with his men. He went to the front door and spoke to a young *bruja* that he knew named Costa.

"Ah, it is you, hombre. What do you need?" asked the short Mexican woman, who came to the door wrapped in a blanket.

"A place to meet with some *amigos* that is out of the way."

"I have a camp in the hills. I take men there who fear gossip to tell on their messing around with a *puta*. No one has ever found it."

"Draw me a map. I need to rent it."

She smiled seductively at him, then went for a blank yellow page and a pencil. With the wall for a desk, she drew a map while she told him of a crossing ahead. Ride west and go up the Baldy Road to a trail marked with a red rag. Then ride around the mountain to a place sheltered by foliage and with a good spring.

He noted while she was drawing how the blanket fell open and exposed her nakedness.

"How do you keep others away?" he asked.

"It has many signs that the devil resides in there."

He laughed. "I bet that does keep them away. It may keep my men away."

She wrinkled her nose at such a thing. Then she shrugged her shoulders and the blanket collapsed at her feet. Her arms went around his neck. "Now I want my rent."

"Darling, I need to find my men." He hugged and kissed her, with her tight boobs pressed hard against him. "Can you have a fiesta down there tonight?"

"How many?"

"Five of us."

"I can't find that many great *putas*, but I will find some sweet ones, and bring a feast of food and wine. That be all right?"

"How much?"

"Thirty pesos."

He dug out the money and paid her. She smiled at him with a threatening frown. "We can finish this tonight," he said.

"You better remember too."

"No problem."

One more hot kiss and he went for his horse. Her words came to his ear as he mounted up: "Don't you forget. Tonight you are mine."

He nodded, waved, and went to find his crew. They needed a great fiesta night before they struck out for the raid. It would make them more of a unit, knowing each other better after sharing a great evening together. Costa knew how to entertain them—they'd all be pleased.

He found Ken on the road an hour later and told him to get the Kid and how to find the hideout.

"Don't worry about all the things to spook you away. Just meet us there."

"I'll get the Kid. We will head up there right now."

"Good. I have two more to find and I will be along." He looked around to be certain they were alone. "We're planning a real fiesta for tonight."

"I won't tell him and he can be surprised." Ken laughed. And then he spurred his horse away. A half hour later Gordon and Charlie Horse found Slocum.

"I have us a hideaway, follow me," Slocum said after they shook hands.

They rode swiftly for the trail marked by a tree trunk wearing a dress, with the model of a woman cut into it, with boobs and a skeleton face. It was gruesome enough to turn back any superstitious person.

They chuckled about real skulls hanging down from trees, so close to a man's face riding by on a horse. Grave markers all along the way and black-cloaked dummies swaying in the gentle wind.

"It sure ain't a place most folks would come by." Gordon's loud laughter echoed through the forest of pines.

They soon saw the horses of the other two men and the high-peaked thatched roof of the shelter. Obviously Costa had not yet made it, but it was mid-afternoon and she had lots to gather.

The Kid stood rolling a cigarette, with his butt to the hitch rail. "Spookiest place I ever been. When do the gawdamn witches arrive?"

"Safest place you have ever been," Slocum said as he dismounted. "Anyone started the beans cooking?"

The Kid shook his head, licked the paper, rolled it up, then with a kitchen match lighted it, and went to puffing. "Hell, any old cantina would have been better than this godforsaken place."

"Kid, build a fire," Ken said, sober-faced. "If we're going to eat tonight, we better get to boiling beans."

The rest didn't know better, and he had no more than got them started cooking than Costa and two beautiful girls rode in on burros with a loaded pack string behind them.

"Hi, hombres. This Rita she has the biggest tits, no?" Costa asked them.

Rita bowed, and then she threw her long hair back and shook her boobs. The men applauded.

"Next is dear Maria. She is hotter than firecracker, no?" Maria made her presentation to them—a shorter, slimmer girl but nonetheless sexy.

"I am Costa and also very hot, huh?" She wiggled her butt and bust at them.

They applauded.

Slocum pointed and named his men to the women.

Then Costa told them, "We are here to have a grand time, but you must wait until I have the food cooked before you get serious with one of us. Savvy?"

"Yes."

"Good. So don't distract them too much from cooking and making tortillas. You can dance and do what you like to do after the meal is prepared and eaten."

The men all agreed. They helped the women unload their donkeys, build bigger fires, and set things out. With his arms filled, the Kid came over and laughed. "I thought this was going to be a fart party for us tonight. You did good, Slocum. Real good."

Costa was cooking a pile of steak strips, sweet peppers, and sliced onion on a grill over the fire. The aroma of her cooking was wonderful and drew the saliva in Slocum's mouth. He went by her where she was bent over and stirring them. Familiarly, he rubbed his hand over her butt. "You did great, girl. This will be a good party for them."

"I do know how to do this." She winked at him.

"You are the best. Have enough money for them too?"

"They can tip the girls, but they are paid."

"I will pass the word."

"That would be nice."

"No problem."

The men were drinking red wine and toasting each other. The good spirits put everyone in a party mood. The wine only fired them up more to have fun and also relaxed them from the serious mission they faced in the next days. Things were unfolding as places were set and men were told if they had plates to go get them—Costa was ready to feed them.

Chinese candles lighted the shelter and the girls were kissy faced with the men as they served from the platters piled high with food and the stack of flour tortillas the two girls had patted out and cooked on a metal sheet.

Everyone pitched in raising a cup of wine to toast the women for their hard work. It was great seeing the enthusiasm they showed filling the plates and passing them on.

Slocum's first bite of the rolled-up tortilla full of meat, peppers, and onions was so good he thought he'd savor it forever. He could not recall eating such good rich food in a long time. He'd almost stay with Costa on a full-time basis just to eat her food.

Then Maria began to play her guitar, and the other two got men up to dance. They finished and others danced with them, while the first went back to eat and drink more wine. Soon Rita went back to a hammock in the dark shadows to entertain the Kid. It was not long before they returned, him to eat and drink more and her to take Ken with her. The night went on, until Costa took Slocum back there.

"Now it is your turn, big hombre," she whispered in his ear.

They climbed in the hammock for a brief encounter, and then she rose to dress.

"A job well done," she whispered in his ear. Then she smothered him with hot kisses and drove her boobs into his bare chest. What a wild fantastic woman.

The music, soft and fast, kept the party going as they switched musicians. Slocum talked with Gordon about his plans for the raid.

"They have an armory just inside the casa. I want to blow it up. Just as soon as that happens, then you and Ken each need to throw a blasting-powder stick grenade, lighted, into his barracks. I hope the explosion at the casa takes care of Gomez and anyone in there. The Kid can watch for anyone escaping the casa. Post him on that rise east of it. You and Ken do the same at the barracks. No one has to live. It should be over in thirty minutes if all goes well."

Gordon nodded. "If we can get there and no one sounds an alarm, it will work."

"You had one of the women?"

"They are tempting as hell, but you know I love that woman at home. She and I don't have any kids, but it damn sure isn't because we ain't tried. She divorced her husband because he wanted more wives. She faced being shunned by her own people over her choice. I was shot up bad when I fell off my horse near her house. She took me in, nursed me back to health, and I told her I was Catholic but I wanted to marry her. She said she was Mormon, but she'd marry me by a justice of the peace only if I simply didn't want more than one wife."

Slocum chuckled. "I knew you had a strong a marriage."

Gordon shook his head as if in dismay. "I never had a woman sweeter to me. She never says no. We can be sweaty working hard together and I can meet her gaze and smile. She'll say 'Now?' And she'll do any wild thing I want to do and laugh about it afterward. Is that a good woman?"

"I knew you were settled, but no man I know still has a honeymoon after ten years."

"Seven glorious years going on eight." Gordon nodded. "I thank heaven every day."

Slocum could see his willowy woman standing with her huge man. They were at ease with each other. He'd had only a vague idea of how they met, but him being shot up and her caring for him was a good story, of two grown-ups thrown together and making a compact to please each other in a marriage.

"I'm ready to turn in," Slocum said. "We will split up to gather again down there tomorrow evening and then strike in the early morning. This man has a bad reputation both here and in raids across the border. He is a bully and a cruel one, I understand. The Federales have not touched him. Dan has many friends on both sides of the border that have been hurt by him, plus he stole some of his cattle. He wanted him put down, but the Apaches are still on the warpath, so he couldn't come with them threatening his ranch."

"I see. I didn't know what you planned exactly, but I knew I must ride with you. Twice before we solved some bad deal like this Gomez. I would have rode with you anywhere."

"I appreciate that and I count on your steady ways to continue."

"Sure. Good night."

"Yes." He shook Gordon's hand.

There were many questions about tomorrow when he left his partners to finish the wine. He planned to leave the pack-horses. In the next twenty-four hours they must move fast to join up outside the Gomez property, then swoop in on them at night and before daybreak blow them away.

He gave each man a different route to get there and exactly where they would meet in late afternoon. They all agreed. The meeting spot he'd chosen was well removed, so they should not be in the sight of anyone.

They split up and headed south one at time. Slocum was last to leave. Passing all the signs of the devil going out, he hoped he had the other side with him. They damn sure had raised hell back there.

7

Slocum crossed a small range of desert mountains on a trail that had been shown to him by a Yaqui Indian on a trip he made to leave Mexico unseen, after a collision with some crooked authorities. He later returned and had them all ousted and sent to prison.

His partners were taking different routes to meet at Lanya Montoya's ranch, which was near Gomez's hacienda. She would say, "You are meeting who here? . . . Oh, yes, I know him. Is he coming? . . . Good. Make yourself at home here."

The fiery redhead would give him hell when he got there.

The way he went was longer, but few could have known the way he used, out of necessity. He watered his horse at some public wells in small towns. They had all been made up as fortresses, to hold out the Apache raiders that once roamed all northern Mexico. Slocum drew some attention, but he just smiled and rode on.

He arrived at Lanya's ranch, and she burst out of her jacal

to demand who he thought he was sending all these horny
men to see her.

"You ain't on your back now." He laughed hard at her
complaining, then kissed and hugged her. "How many are
here?"

"A damn army of them. Did you say I'd do them all?"

"Whatever they said." He put his arm over her shoulder
and herded her toward the men.

"Did you all meet this lovely lady Lanya?"

"Yes, sir," Ken said

"Good. If she has enough food, she will feed us."

"If I am going to feed you, then I need some goats killed
for supper."

Ken rose. "Point them out. They will be skinned and
dressed in ten minutes."

She smiled. "You from Texas?"

"Yes, ma'am. And I have butchered a thousand goats
growing up."

"Excuse me." She disengaged from Slocum and went to
show him her choices and the ropes to hang them from, and
then told the Kid to get some buckets of water from her well.
He and Gordon went to get them. Charlie helped Ken, grab-
bing the goats by one hind leg and dragging the bleating
ones to slaughter.

Lanya ran to get them her knives. Slocum held a bleating
goat by the leg while Charlie went for the last one.

Ken stunned the first one with a hammer, knocking him
unconscious. Charlie handed his to Slocum to hold and then
helped him hang it by putting the goat's back legs in the
loops. Ken cut that goats' throats to bleed them out. Then
with a very sharp pocketknife he began to take the hides
off, making his cuts from underneath.

The Kid blinked at his method. "Why you doing that?"

"So I don't get cut hair all over him. My dad said to do

that, and we'd get a kick in the butt if we laid an unwashed hand on the meat too. You don't want that flavor on the meat."

"You do that on a deer too?" the Kid asked.

"Hell yeah."

"I bet that works."

Ken agreed. "It damn sure does."

"I'll watch and do it that way from now on."

The Kid and Charlie doused the goats down with buckets of water while the others washed up.

"You need them cut up?" Ken asked Lanya.

"I could use some help. You guys are damn good. Bring them to the kitchen meanwhile. I can fry the livers with onions and serve them for your snacks."

"We're coming," Slocum said with one carcass on his shoulder.

The goats were finally cooked, and served along with red wine, tortillas, and beans; they ate well. Then they slept a few hours and saddled up under the stars. Everyone rechecked his weapons and the bombs made to blow things up at Gomez's place. Each "bomb" consisted three sticks of blasting powder tied securely together, with a long fuse that could be shortened if necessary.

"That fuse takes four minutes to burn down. You can figure the rest," Slocum told Ken and Gordon, who would handle the barracks. He and Charlie would deliver the armory explosion. He kissed Lanya good-bye, paid her forty dollars, which made her smile, and they rode eastward for the hacienda.

They arrived at four A.M. Charlie was beside Slocum as they made their way carefully to the house. The other three rode wide of it. The main guard was at the gate—the position once held by the horny one Roma had screwed for him while he inspected the house. Would they have more than one guard now that they knew they'd been breached for some reason?

On his belly, Slocum could only see one guard pacing around the gate in the darkness. When the guard walked north, Charlie knelt down on one knee and drew back his bow with the long arrow in place. When the guard turned back, the arrow took swift flight and struck him squarely in the chest. He managed only a grunt and fell facedown on the ground, unable to warn anyone.

The two ran past the guard's quivering boots as he went through the last trauma before death. Slocum slid the gate open slowly with hardly a sound. Across the courtyard they ran to the front door, and to Slocum's relief, it opened. Then they were in the chamber with the armory on the right. He opened the door, and from a high window starlight shone in on all the guns, rockets, and other equipment for war.

He lighted a match and so did Charlie. Fuses lit and sparkling, they tossed their bombs high on the stacks. Then they hurried out, and were a hundred yards away when the gigantic explosion blew the high tile roof off that portion of the house and more ammo went off too. Two minutes later, *bam, bam*, two more explosions followed.

"Good," Slocum said to Charlie. "That's the barracks."

The raging fire consuming the casa shed light for a quarter mile around the place. Slocum drew up beside the Kid on the ridge.

"See anyone escape?"

"Hell no, and they won't, or I'll kill them. You see that roof explode? Whew! That was bigger than Fourth of July fireworks."

"Keep watching," Slocum told him, then rode on to find Gordon and Ken.

The barracks were in a raging fire as well. Dying men trapped inside were screaming, but none emerged from the orange glow of raging fire. Soon only the roar and crackle of the fire could be heard.

Gordon rode over with Slocum. "What if he wasn't inside there?"

"We must wait and see. We should know today."

"Where will we find food today?"

"There is a small village nearby, where Roma is, the woman who lost her eye helping me. I can check on her while we are there."

"How much longer should we watch for them escaping?"

"Another hour. I sure hope we've got him. He won't do much plundering and raiding anyhow if he did survive."

Gordon shook his head.

They left the still-burning hacienda and rode to the village. A few street vendors made the men food and then they split up. Slocum had gone to the doctor's house, and there he found a happy Roma, with a patch over her absent eye, rocking on the porch.

"Word is that bastard is gone," she said, standing up and walking down using the handrail. "I am still dizzy. They say it will improve. Will you hold me?"

"Sure. I am glad you are recovering." He held her to his chest.

"Señor Wade wants me to move into his casa. Should I go?"

"Only you can answer that. You know I am not a post that will be here for you."

"I know, but I enjoyed my freedom. If I go there, I will have to fit his mold."

"He has luxury you can't find in this land."

"I know, but I don't value that as much as I do having my freedom to choose who I want and what I want to do. Like when I met you—I could have been stuck there, living there.

I had fun riding with you until the end, and you could not have stopped that."

"But today unfortunately you are weaker and more vulnerable."

"I know. Did you end that bastard?"

"I think so. At least he has no guns and ammo."

"Where will you go?"

He gave her a head toss north.

"God be with you, big man. Walk me up the steps. I feel a little dizzy."

He swept her up in his arms and carried her back up. "You want back inside or in the rocker?"

"Rocker."

He put her down on her feet and she sat down.

"Thanks. They treat me nice here. He looks out for me. I will be fine even one-eyed."

He left her and rejoined his men. "Any word if he was away from the hacienda?"

They all shook their heads.

"How much time should we give it?" Ken asked.

"We can go through the ashes looking for bodies when things cool down."

"We need to go back there now?" Ken asked

"Yes. Scavengers will be there, with the buzzards."

"Should we buy some food to cook?" he asked.

"I guess. Our packhorses are a ways away. Get some firewood peddlers and some of these street vendors to go up there. You see they get food to take along. I will pay them well for the move. I must go see a man, and then I will join you at the hacienda."

The men agreed and set out to get it done. Slocum rode up the hill to Martin Wade's casa to have a talk with him. The very idea that Gomez might not have been in the house ate at him. There needed to be a positive sign he was no longer alive.

Wade met him at the gate when the guard had let him in and a groom had taken his horse. "Well, I hear the country has been relieved of a problem."

"I hope so. No one is certain he was in the fire."

"Come in. You had lunch?"

"No. I didn't take time. I knew you had contacts. Keep me informed if you learn anything. I will be out there at the hacienda to check if we can find any remains."

"I will have some lunch readied for you. Did you see my good friend today?"

"Yes, she is still very weak. Dizzy she said."

"Oh, she is stronger than she was. But not well yet, I agree. I hope she makes up her mind to come here when she is stronger."

Slocum dropped in a chair he showed him. "She has to make up her mind, and it isn't straight thinking yet."

Wade agreed.

His housekeeper brought Slocum some sopapillas and coffee. "The food is being fixed," she said.

He thanked her and turned back to Wade. "We couldn't be exposed checking on Gomez's location before we made the raid, and we had no information."

"Where could he be?"

"If he got word we were coming, he might have not taken a chance, since our spy operation had been discovered. I simply don't know, but it bothers the hell out of me. Time will tell, I guess."

His food arrived, served on a tray the woman set before him.

"Can I get you fresh soapapillas?" she asked him.

"No, I'm fine. Thank you."

She brought more out regardless of his protesting.

Wade laughed. "She's hard of hearing," he said and then he snickered. "And fussy."

After his meal, Slocum rode back to the hacienda and joined his men.

"The Kid's gone back for the packhorses," Ken said. "The ashes are still too hot to search the house. I don't know—it all collapsed in so much, so what's left of him might be just that—ashes."

"That's fine."

"I talked to some peons who worked around here for him, and they think he was in the casa last night," Gordon said.

"Good. We'll find out."

"What else can we do?"

"Nothing but wait and see."

"Several widows of the men killed in the blast are here crying. They don't know if he was in bed in there or not."

Slocum agreed with the big man. Wait and see if maybe someone would come forward and tell them either way. Late evening the Kid came back with the packhorses. Everyone went to help him unload the animals.

"You learn anything?" Slocum asked.

"Maybe, I don't know. I bought supper from an old *bruja* in a village near the hideout. She said Gomez had a woman in San Pedro he slept with often."

"You get her name?"

The Kid shook his head. "No, she wouldn't tell me."

"What was that?" Gordon asked, and Ken also joined them

"The Kid says an old woman told him Gomez had a woman in San Pedro he slept with often."

"Was he with her last night?" Ken asked.

Slocum shook his head. "She wouldn't say. Only that he slept there often."

The Kid agreed, taking off his own saddle. "I couldn't even buy her name."

"A couple of us need to ride down there. If he's using a *puta* down there or a woman who lives there, a few pesos should buy that information off of *someone*." Slocum was convinced that would settle the deal. Who should go?

"Ken, you and the Kid go see what you can find out. Some bartender or storekeeper will tell you all about his affair for a few pesos. We are only needing to know if he was here or there."

The Kid swung his saddle back on his horse. "That old *bruja* won't tell us, but I bet someone will, like you say. Money makes 'em talk."

"Be careful. If he's still alive he may have a henchman with him, and he could be like a sidewinder, aroused enough to strike, and hard."

Ken agreed. "We'll see, and we'll watch our backs."

"Meanwhile we'll check around here. We need him removed from his place of power." Slocum gave them money to bribe with and to eat on. They soon rode out, and he shook his head. Why was it so damn hard to find out if the outlaw had perished in the fire or was still alive?

If he was alive, Gomez was not going to show his face until he had enough force to fight them. And the Federales might get interested in the destruction of the hacienda and come see who did it. They needed to be ready to ride off if they were threatened in either case. His handful of men with stealth had wiped out Gomez's base of power, but they were too small for a full-scale, out-and-out war.

"You need some sleep," Gordon said to Slocum. "Charlie is surveying things around the area, looking out for any force or group that might be sent here."

"Good. I will take a siesta, but don't let me sleep over four hours."

"Why don't you use the hammock out back in the shade? I'll be here and awake."

Slocum shook his head. "You know I like things resolved. We damn sure don't have this one done, or at least we don't know if we do."

"I will get you up if I learn one thing."

"Good."

Sleep didn't come easy, but he soon fell off into troubled slumber.

8

"Better wake up," Gordon said. "The men are back from San Pedro and they don't have good news."

Trying to clear the sleep away in the light of sundown, Slocum blinked at Ken and the Kid.

"What went on?"

"We found and talked to his concubine, a woman called Leona," Ken said. "She said that after sunup today, a man came and got him out of her bed, and he went with him," Ken said.

"Damn. Kid, you did a good job finding out about her. You two found her and I trust you feel she told the truth."

Ken and the Kid agreed.

"Then we need to find his trail. We came to destroy him. We need to do our damndest to do that or he will rebuild all we've destroyed and hurt more people doing it. Check our supplies. We need to start down there and begin trailing him at dawn."

His men nodded somberly.

"Charlie, tomorrow we'll need to pick up whatever dim trail he left us."

He nodded. "We will find him."

"Now we know he is alive, I agree he can't hide anywhere we can't find him."

Slocum now felt they'd wasted two days, but if Gomez still breathed, they had a job now to try and get him again.

Mid-morning they were in San Pedro. While the others got food in a local cantina, Slocum flipped a ten-dollar gold piece in the air, gleaming and polished in the sun, around the women busy washing clothes at the end of the village trough.

One of the women bent over and shook her ass at him. "You want me, hombre?"

They laughed. Some of the women went red-faced at her words.

"Gomez was here two nights ago. Where did he go to hide?"

Some women shrugged. Others made faces that said they did not want to be a part of it. One woman swept her hair back and rose up from scrubbing clothes; her dollar-size nipples showed under the thin, wet dress material. "How much would you pay me to tell you where he went?"

"Twenty pesos."

"For that much I would service you and all your brothers."

The women laughed.

"My brothers are fine. Where did he go?" Slocum asked her, getting out the second coin.

"Twenty pesos."

"I have it right here."

"He went to his ranch."

"No, it had been totally destroyed."

"We heard that. But no, he has a ranch in the Madres."

"How do you know that?"

"He took me there once."

The washerwomen all looked hard at her.

She handed her wet clothes to a woman beside her and approached Slocum.

Under his breath, he asked an older woman who knelt beside him, "Does she tell the truth?"

"She may. She was very wild as a girl."

"What is your name?" he asked the approaching woman.

"Silva, what is yours?"

"Slocum. How much to lead us to this place?"

She folded her arms over her chest. "A hundred pesos and a good horse to ride home."

She was maybe four feet, three inches tall, with slim hips, and she'd put her long hair in a ponytail. Probably mid-twenties, and she spoke out clear and straight-sounding.

"Can you leave right now?"

"Sure, why not?"

"You have a family and a husband?"

"He can watch the kids. My sister will help him, she is a widow. I can go."

He turned and mounted his horse. Once in the saddle, he bent over, pulled her up, and swung her behind him like a feather. It wasn't her first time to get on a horse like that. Her bare legs looked shapely when she scooted up to him. With no hesitation she threw her hands around him, clamped them on his belly, and buried her boobs in his back.

"I am ready, hombre."

He reined the pacing horse around and rode out over to the cantina. He stopped his mount and shouted, "Mount up. We're leaving."

His men filed out, smiled at Silva, unhitched their horses, and mounted.

Slocum turned his horse. "Silva is going to take us to him."

The men nodded at her, turned their horses, and together they all left the village.

"Tough men ride with you," Silva said, peering around at them.

Slocum agreed. "They're tough men."

"Are you going to kill Gomez?"

"If we can find him. Did you have an affair with him at one time?"

"Yes. I was young and foolish. I thought he would shed his wife and put me in the hacienda casa."

"He didn't do that of course?"

She leaned forward beside him to tell her story, "No, he used me, and when he was through his boy used me. So when I was six months pregnant and big as a bear, they took me out in the desert and told me to go home."

"Did you go home?"

"Of course not. I had diseases in my womanhood and was too dumb from being on dope they gave me so that I did not scream when they touched me. A good *bruja* took me in, and her medicine cured the diseases I had down there. Then she cured my addiction to the drugs they gave me. But my twins died at birth. I had to get over that myself. But a man twenty years older married me and we have two children. We have no money. He is kind. My sister who is a widow, she will tend my children and her two and him as well."

"What killed her man?"

"He got sick and died. The doctor said he had a high fever. He had no answer. The *bruja* who saved me could have cured him, but I could not find her. Lucky we all did not get it."

Slocum agreed. Many diseases that made people sick no one could cure.

They made camp on a small river under some cottonwoods. The men brought Silva wood for a fire. From the pannier supplies, she made bread they cooked on sticks. It was good if you did not burn it, Slocum decided, and he ate several dough balls cooked on the flames. Later, when the beans were well cooked, she fed them. Her coffee was strong, but it cleared Slocum's mind after all his days in the saddle.

She sat beside him on a log, her dress pulled up so her knees were exposed. In the firelight she drew things with a stick in the dirt between her bare feet. Slocum studied her work. The first thing she drew was a mare squatted down. Very real. Then she drew a stallion mounted on her and his dick in her. He could imagine them on canvas—perhaps in charcoal or oils; she could probably sell the picture in certain markets.

"What do you do with your art?"

"Make impressions for people."

"Impressions of what?"

"What that horse is doing to that mare."

He noticed they were alone. The other men, obviously tired from the long ride, had slipped away. They'd spend some long days ahead too if they were ever going to reach the mountains and then find Gomez's ranchero.

"What you are going to do to me?" she quietly asked him.

He blinked at her. "Why me?"

"I have seen you maybe a half dozen times in Mexico. And I would say, 'There is a big gringo hombre. I would like to have him one day for myself. What is his name?' No one I asked knew your name. Then last fall you were at the Blanco Springs with a pack train and some more pistoleros."

"We had some newly minted coins from the Silver City mint to deliver in Guaymas."

She raised her head a little haughtily. "Then before I could get to you, a blonde rode up on a gray horse and took you away."

"Donna Logan was her name."

"I did not care. She was just another *puta* to me. And today I am dressed in a wash-worn dress that my nipples show through and my hair isn't half as nice as hers was. I had not fixed it, and I have no brush to do it with or better clothing to wear. I probably stink like the lye soap I used on his underwear. But I was dressed nice at Blanco. So"—she stretched her hands over her head—"I would still love to fuck you tonight."

"I bet we've got time. What did you do at Blanco Springs?"

"I am glad you have time. I took a man some wine we made. My husband has grapes and trees. He makes wine. I took some to a rich man who lives up there. My husband thinks the old man likes his wine and pays him a good price for it. But it is because I deliver it to him. What did you do with the blond girl that night?"

He leaned over and whispered in her ear. "What I am going to do to you—later."

"How much later?"

"This ranchero of his, you can lead us there?"

She frowned in the starlight. "I told you I could. I have been there several times. One of his young men would come get me at the village. Bring me on a fine horse, buy me meals, and be sure I slept alone and no one touched me. At the ranchero, I would wait for Gomez to come. I would get bored. Then he would come and we'd have wild times. He would say he loved me and I should be his wife. Then one night he would be gone and I'd wake up. Then that nice boy told me that I was his and he'd jump in bed and screw me silly. Then he would drug me enough that I could not fight him. After that he'd take me home on a roundabout way and he would screw me all the time we traveled.

"I would live on the money the boy paid me, and then he would come and make me undress. Then when he was satisfied, he took me back and never touched me going up there. Gomez and I partied for two weeks. He was gone the next morning and left me a pouch of money.

"That boy came and he screwed me and said he was taking me home. I let him. It was that or be roughly raped. We started for home. He was standing on the edge of this cliff pissing off on the first day. Before he was done, I reached around to hold his cock.

"'Let me make it hard,' I said. I began to pull on it and his dick began to harden and him breathing harder. I whispered, 'Are you ready to go fuck her?'

"He said, 'Sure. Who?'

"Then with both hands I shoved him off the cliff. 'Here she is!' I said. 'You horny bastard.'

"He fell for hundreds of feet and I went home with three horses. His, the packhorse, and mine."

"Did they do anything to you?"

"Gomez must have figured it out. He sent a new boy to take me up there, one who knew nothing and treated me nice. But Gomez acted mean and different to me. He doped me and demanded to know where his son's body was at. He even beat me with a whip, and in the end of his torture, I still said, 'He fell off the mountain. I am not lying.'

"I told him he fell off the mountain walking around his horse. I had no way to get him a message. I never knew that was his son. But he gave me to his man when he left, and that bastard chained me to the bed. He left me to four of his men who used me. I had to escape, and I did it by pouring laudanum in their beer when they were drunk, then I took a horse and left.

"That *bruja* found me, hid me from his men looking for me, and she cured me—but the twins died—I told you that."

"That's terrible."

She scuffed the drawing out with her sole.

"Why do that?"

"I drew that picture for you. I don't want those others to think I did it for them."

They went a short distance from the camp. With the side of his boot, he cleared out any rocks on the sandy creek-bank ground. Then he spread out bedrolls for the two of them and they settled down for the evening.

She woke him before dawn with "Hurry, get up. I must make breakfast for the men."

She ran off to the creek to bathe, then came back and started the fire. Her dress was still not dry and it clung to her. But she worked hard and soon was making flour torti-llas between her palms to go with reheated beans and fried bacon.

Her tortillas made, she cooked down some dried apples, brown sugar, and raisins, which she wrapped in the tortillas and gave to the men for desert. They all bragged on her.

"Next town is Bronco Nigra. I want a nice slab of beef, some cilantro, some sweet peppers and onions. We will have a fiesta tonight," she said.

"I'll love that," Gordon said. "And ain't even smelled it cooking yet."

They all laughed.

"How much farther is it to the ranchero?" Ken asked her.

"Two days we will be at the base of the mountains. I told Slocum I have been there several times. From the base it takes a day and a half to get up there."

He saluted her. "Good. I simply wanted to know."

They rode to Bronco Nigra, where Slocum saw no black horses like the ones they said Gomez rode. The butcher cut him out a nice chunk of beef, and charged him enough to pay for the hanging steer. The rest of the items Silva bought from the women selling produce.

Slocum stopped her. "Would that woman's dress fit you?"

The woman was close to Silva's size.

"I think it would." She went over and backed up to the other woman's butt. The dress owner acted shocked when Silva said, "It would fit me."

"I want to buy your dress for five pesos. Here is the money; take it off. You can wear her dress home."

"Here?" She looked shocked and embarrassed.

"I won't look," he said and turned his back to her.

The other market women ran over and told her, "Take it off. Take it off. You can make a half dozen more for that much money."

He heard her say at last, "All right." And he turned around in time to see her bare boobs and naked belly as she put on Silva's old dress. Silva had a lot cuter figure, naked just now as she put her new dress on over her head and wiggled it down. He paid the woman for the dress and fended off several offers from others to sell him their dresses. He shook his head thanked them and they rode on.

Silva laughed. "That girl was about too embarrassed to talk even about trading it. She thought you wanted to screw her, I bet. Hell I have been paid less by dirty old men to stay for three days with them."

"Caught her way off guard."

"Five pesos for one dress. You really helped her out a lot."

That evening they had thin strips of meat browned over mesquite, then fried with onions, sweet peppers, and cilantro. Silva made stacks of flour tortillas on a grill.

Enough beans were made to have with the tortillas and still leave some to have for breakfast. They feasted on Silva's meal and ate till they were bloated. She put what was left of the beans in a pot, put a cover on it, and stoked enough ashes to keep it warm all night. Then she took Slocum's bedroll up the way, while his men talked about being careful in the days ahead on the trail.

When he went to slip off his boots and undress, he could tell she was crying. Lifting the cover, he leaned over and asked, "What is wrong?"

"No one ever did anything that nice for me in my whole life. I couldn't believe you'd ask her for that dress that she wore right there and then have her take it off too. It is such a beautiful dress. I hate to wear it out here. I may never own another that good."

"Don't cry over that. You can cry," he whispered, "about sad things."

Crazy Mexican women, he loved them all. Hell, he loved most women, but the Spanish were the fieriest of them all in bed with a dick inside them. Whew, what a woman!

The next morning the two of them beat the sunrise to get up. Then she went down and bathed but left her dress on the bank this time, used a towel to dry, then wiggled into the dress. He squatted on the bank to watch her in the starlight. He liked to watch her do that.

She made fresh tortillas with last night's leftovers. Slocum's men staggered awake and in the cool pink light of predawn came and filled their cups with her coffee.

"I bet your husband misses you," Ken said in a dry precoffee voice.

"No, my sister the widow cares for him when I am gone." She laughed, tossing the sheet of flour and lard up in the air.

"She cares for him?"

"Sure, he is sweet to us both. Lenore is a woman—she needs attention too."

"Damn he's lucky."

"So are we, hombre. So are we."

"I see the Sierra Madre outline this morning. You told us two days. Thanks for helping and feeding us."

"You are fun to feed all of you."

"Do you suppose he has scouts around here watching for men like us?" Slocum asked, coffee cup in his hand and sitting on his boot heels.

She drew a deep breath and chewed on her lower lip before she said, "He must know about his hacienda burning down and the loss of his men. He could have lookouts."

Slocum agreed and told the men they needed to be close to their guns. They packed up after breakfast and headed on the road to the mountains that loomed more and more all day.

In a small settlement with a church he found her another butcher, who cut her meat. She bought more produce from women there. Before they left to catch the men, she told Slocum she wished to buy a candle and pray for their safety. He loaned her his silk kerchief to wear for a scarf on her head. She went inside the church, touched the holy water to her forehead, and crossed herself, then genuflected. She did it again at the line of small candles burning at the front near the altar. She placed the one she'd bought beside them and lit it.

At the rail she knelt and prayed for a short while, crossed herself again, and then hurried back to him standing hatless in the entranceway. Outside he replaced his hat and the kerchief she handed him under the noisy birds in the cottonwood trees.

"Better now?"

"I should have confessed my sins, but you didn't have all day."

"I bet he forgives you."

"He's a man, isn't he?"

Slocum chuckled. "I guess he is."

"Good men forgive you, bad men beat and hurt you over nothing."

He swung into the saddle. "I must be good."

"Oh, Slocum you are a great good man. I don't want to think this will be over in a few days."

They hurried to catch the others.

Slocum took a bath in the stream that evening before they went to bed. The mountain-base water was colder than that behind them. She shaved him and in the bedroll they had sex.

Afterward he lay back and thought about trips he'd made in and out of these great mountains. With Tom Horn the army scout and a dozen Chiricahua Apaches. Tom had lived with a squaw from their tribe in the White Mountains for several years. He knew what they thought. He spoke their language. Many said he should have been in charge instead of Al Sieber. He found two chiefs, Mano and Clell, and talked them and their people into coming back with them. But when they broke up the reservation, they sent them to San Carlos, and they all went back to Mexico. Tom blamed that on a know-it-all son of a bitch they put in charge who later quit the Indian service to run a newspaper in Tombstone. Tom could talk all day about the mess they'd made of the whole Apache deal. San Carlos was the last and worst asshole of the world. Saguaro cactus didn't even grow there.

Charlie Horse woke him in the night. "Quiet. There are some men around us. I think they plan to kill us at daylight. I will wake the others and tell them," he whispered.

"Tell them to keep low and get away from their bedrolls. We may be able to kill some before the sun even lights the sky."

Silva gripped his arm. "I didn't lead you into a trap."

"Glad you prayed. May have saved us. Now, real quiet, slip over to our left and lay down beside that fallen tree. But move slow and careful." She nodded, and threw over herself a dark blanket like the ones Plains Indians used as a buffalo robe, to hide under if she could get close enough to kill one of the intruders

She was in place. With his pants on, Slocum still was in the bedroll. Six-gun in his fist, he eased out of the sleeping bag on all fours and made his way to a large gnarled tree trunk. A man out in the night coughed. Then Slocum heard the quick whisp of an arrow, and another unseen man, farther down, screamed. Guns blazed, but they were not close enough to the camp. The orange flame of their barrels only made targets his men answered.

Then silence. Another man screamed down by the stream, then the splash of a body hit the water. Slocum knew the sound of his cry. A knife blade had found his back.

"They are disarmed," Ken shouted. "Anyone hurt?"

Slocum sat down and put on his socks and boots, after dumping them to make sure no scorpion was inside. He also wiped off his soles first, so no sticklers were stuck in his feet.

"I'm okay," the Kid said. "Thanks, Charlie Horse."

"Yeah, thanks," Gordon said.

"The one in the river is dead," Ken said. Slocum decided he must have been wading out of the water.

"Charlie, you all right?" he called out.

"I am fine. But there are none of them alive now. What will we do with them?"

"Drag them across the stream by horseback and cave a bank on them over where that dry wash joins the river."

"Thank God," the Kid said. "I thought Slocum would want them buried."

They all laughed. Silva got dressed and shook her head. "I must go to church more often."

"Yes. All over." He hugged and kissed her to reassure her that it was indeed over, for then anyway.

The bodies buried, they rounded up their attackers' horses to take along. Gordon picked a big roan horse from them to ride himself. His horse was weary from packing him, he said. Slocum agreed. They found a total of seventy-six dollars on the men. They gave that to Silva, and she couldn't believe they had done that.

"*Gracias, amigos.* You all are too sweet to me," she said. "But now I must ride a horse and can no longer hug him," she added, gesturing toward Slocum.

They laughed at her and each man hugged and kissed her. Then they loaded up and rode on.

Slocum knew they needed to post guards each night. There were five dead men less to worry about anyway. Gomez might be gathering a new army, but he wouldn't find many in the mountains—he would have to recruit them in the flatlands. He would need guns and ammo, plus horses for most that he hired, and food, plus he'd need to get some *putas* up there to keep the men around camp. He'd be a while doing all that. Plus he would need money too. Slocum figured his last fortune had gone up in smoke at the hacienda fire sale.

They needed to cut him out before he got the plan going. In the saddle as the tough pacing horse pulled the steep trail hard, already the air was cooler and he could smell pines. *Gomez, I am coming.*

9

That afternoon they camped at a large spring with a wide meadow surrounded by pines, with good grass for their animals. Slocum had them clean all the guns they'd taken off the outlaws. That would mean more firepower if they engaged them. The two single-shot rifles were worn out. He put the barrels in a wedge between rocks and bent them, so they could serve no one.

Two good Winchester repeaters that used .44 rimfire ammo were the best catch. Ken and Gordon took them and split the ammunition they'd found. The Kid found a great Bowie knife and practiced throwing it at a pine tree until he could stick it deep in the bark.

The Kid also gave Silva a small .30-caliber Colt. "You can shoot it, Silva. It won't kick much."

"Good. I know how to shoot. *Muchos gracias, hombre.*"

Slocum squatted down beside her making tortillas on her knees. "How far is he from here?"

"Maybe ten miles from here around the mountain one

way; there is trail goes south. He has a big meadow and his place is at the back of it. He can see you coming a half mile away unless you come through the pines. But it would be rugged."

He nodded. "Charlie and I may go scout it out."

"Oh be careful. He is much tougher than those men he sent to kill us."

"I'll be careful."

Next he had a parley with his men over supper.

They were around him in a circle. "Ken, you, Gordon, and the Kid move way down this meadow and build a fort, not too high, with dead logs, but one you can get behind and shoot from. Then you four don't build big cooking fires. But be on guard night and day."

"What are you going to do?" the Kid asked.

"Charlie and I will try to sneak up on Gomez."

"You don't need us?" Gordon asked.

"Not yet. We need to know the layout of his place and how many are up here. You four keep low and don't let them take you asleep."

"We won't," Ken promised him.

They left in the night, when the moon rose. Both he and Charlie chose plain-colored brown horses that might blend better than Slocum's reddish pacing horse and Charlie's black. Two big owls soared through the pines and hooted for each other. Bats came in clouds looking for insects but never bothered them. Silva had told Slocum that large granite boulders were at the entrance to the meadow, and when he found them, he could see beyond them a wide-open silver valley of many acres. They took their horses well back in the woods and tied them so they'd be there when they needed them.

Skirting along the wood's edge, Slocum knew no one could see them, and they went at a lope. He carried his Spencer and Charlie his bow. When they paused to rest and catch their breath, there were no lights on in the low-walled log building and still hours till dawn. Standing in the cool night, he and Charlie skirted the cabin and found a dozen horses in the corral.

Charlie took his knife and almost cut through each girth on the saddles, at the top rail. Slocum approved. There were some rifles in the scabbards. He got mud and jammed the barrels full then wiped the outsides clean and replaced them in the scabbards.

He suspected there might be ten men inside, from the number of saddles. The five they buried had been one-third of Gomez's whole gang. At the moment he wished he'd brought some blasting powder packages along and taken them out right then while they snored. Oh well, better luck next time.

He needed to lure them out into a trap next. Charlie stopped him with his arm out. They both froze as a woman came out, raised her skirt, squatted, and peed, then went back inside, never noticing them behind the corral.

He winked at Charlie. "Let's go."

Back at camp he explained what they'd done and how he and Charlie wanted them to rush out to get at Gomez's men. Then they'd get dumped off their horses or their rifles would blow up in their faces. The rest they could pick off. He and Charlie would be in place to take them if they came back to the ranch house.

Everyone agreed the plan should work. They rested that day, and Slocum took Silva up in the forest away from them, with a blanket to lie on and to make love on as well. A leisurely day to kiss and look at the azure sky above, then have sex.

"Where will you go when this is all over?" she asked.

"Arizona. The Apaches have been raising hell up there. I have a lady I am responsible for who teaches school and may need to go home if things have quieted down."

"Will you marry her?"

"No. I have no casa for a wife. No way to earn a living. I would be a poor choice for a husband. Her husband was killed by bank robbers getting away, and then she learned he had another wife and some children. So she came to teach school out here. I found her in the path of the Apaches and took her to a place to be safe."

On her belly beside him, she smiled and shook her head. "You are a handy man. Does she make good love?"

"No better than you."

"Do you tell all your women that?"

"I don't tell the others anything."

She laughed and then chewed on a grass stem. "I bet you don't."

They took a siesta and afterward went back so she could make supper.

Late in the night, Slocum and Charlie returned to their place at Gomez's ranch. But Slocum only counted eight saddles— no one had changed girths on the saddles, but one Winchester was gone.

Had Gomez and one other slipped away again?

He and Charlie whispered about it when a woman came out. Charlie caught her by the mouth to cut off any screams and they dragged her behind a shed.

"You scared the piss out of me," she whispered angrily.

"How many women are in there?"

"Two more."

"Be quiet and bring them out. But if they wake the men, they will die in there. When you bring them out, go behind this shed and get on the ground. When did Gomez ride out?" Slocum asked.

"Just before those bastards of his raped us."

Good, the women would now have a reason to leave. "Be quiet or die."

She nodded and in the starlight made a face about her wet dress front before she went back inside.

In a short time the three came out. Two were still dressing, and Charlie showed them were to get to.

Angry that his man had escaped him again, Slocum lighted a charge and tossed the bomb inside the door, then ran out back with the crouched women and his man. The explosion blew the sod roof off and rained dirt on them.

"They won't rape anyone again," Slocum said. "We have to fix the saddles before you can use them. Charlie, go get our crew. We missed that bastard again. You ladies can make breakfast for us."

"Who are you?" the sassy one asked.

"My name's Slocum. That's Charlie Horse. There are more coming and another woman."

"Will we be free when this is over?"

"Free as the birds. Why?"

"After how badly they treated us, I am going back to my village and be a wife again."

He laughed. "And the first exciting offer comes along, you will ride away again."

"Not me. I swear to God not ever again." She threw her arms in the air and went with the others to make food.

Charlie had gone to get the rest of their gang.

Slocum went where the women were setting up to cook outside. "Where did he go?"

They shook their heads. "He never said anything," the

leader said, "but his men didn't come back, and it made him mad at all of us. It wasn't our fault they ran away."

"No, they all died charging our camp."

"Good enough for them."

The others agreed.

His crew arrived. Gordon examined the corpses, and the others got all their money—fifty dollars. He paid it to the women, and the men fixed them three girths for them to ride out of there on. Except for the loss of their things in the explosion, they thanked them.

After they ate, Slocum noticed the Kid had convinced Annette to slip off and share her body with him. Everyone was amused. She was the cutest of the three and the least mouthy. Sassy had mentioned to him that Gomez might try to hide at Zamora's camp in the north. Zamora was one of the rebel outlaws that operated out of the mountains and was mostly left alone by Federales because of his fierce defense of his region. Two expeditions by the military had ended in failure and the loss of many soldiers, so Zamora sat like a king in the high country. But whether or not he would hide Gomez was dependent entirely on what Gomez had left to pay him for protection.

Slocum had enough worries about how to find this outlaw. But he wasn't ready to give up. They saddled horses for the girls, and they had enough food from the hideout to make it back to civilization. The women thanked him and his men before they rode out. Slocum decided to leave the unnecessary horses in the meadow, with water and grass, to fend for themselves. A horse herd was hard to move fast.

"You were only a short time from catching him," Silva said.

"If I'd had a bomb with me the night before, he'd be singing in the devil's choir."

"Don't blame yourself," she said, riding close to his left leg. "You will get him. He can't be this lucky for long."

"He must have a bird telling him when we get close."

"His luck will run on. Don't be so upset. You will find a way to catch him."

"I'll be fine, Silva. I intend to run him down."

She shrugged and reined back some.

He turned back and nodded to her. No need in upsetting her; she'd been good inspiration and great company that he appreciated.

Soon they crossed another range. His tracker, Charlie, was satisfied they were getting close to the pair.

So to hurry things Slocum sent him ahead and held up until Charlie had a good start and they fell in behind. His plan was that Gomez might not suspect one rider, who was an Indian. But they didn't catch up with Gomez. Charlie pulled back and reminded Slocum that they were pushing their horses to death and that it would soon be dark. They should close down their pursuit.

Slocum agreed. "Make camp. We'll try again tomorrow." He pointed out a place, and they all agreed.

In his bedroll with him, Silva was naked, resting half on his chest and sipping kisses. "You are sure upset."

"Twice I missed that bastard, and he probably will get away this time." He could hardly stand himself over not getting Gomez.

"I keep saying he can't run away from you. You will get him." She kissed him sweetly.

"Where will he go?"

"I am not sure where he will hide, but you will find him. Now, jack up your tool and get busy. We can't waste tonight."

He clutched her face and kissed her hard. One thing he needed to do was forget Gomez, and she was the prize he could use to get over his depression. They were soon one, and his mind whirled away to savor her passion and his own. This sweet woman who had been through so much herself might pull him out of his own ditch. She completely gave her all to him every time they had sex. Not only willing, but ready, for fierce passion, and able to extract it from him. Did her *older* husband realize what she was? He probably never knew, but she was a gem. He about laughed. She had told them that he had her sister until she got back—he might not even miss her.

In the morning he spoke to the other men. "We may be on a wild-goose chase. I told Dan I'd get him, but the way things look now, so tangled, he may escape us. Any of you want to go home?"

"Hell, no," Ken said, and the rest agreed.

"All right, let's hit the trail."

That evening they reached a small village called Alto. They left Silva and Gordon in camp to watch things. Charlie was off scouting, so Slocum, Ken, and the Kid went to the local cantina and drank some homemade beer. The Kid screwed a young whore there and came back to the table.

In a whisper he said, slipping into the booth, "She said he was here yesterday."

"Did she know where he went?"

His voice still low, he said, "She thinks she can find out. I told her we'd pay her five pesos." The Kid shook his head. "That's a fortune to her."

"How far did she have to go to find out?"

He turned his palms up and shook his head. "I don't know. But it might be a lead."

Ken put his hand on the Kid's shoulder. "Screw another one. Maybe you can learn some more."

Amused, Slocum thanked the Kid. The big man who owned the place was coming with more of his horse piss.

"Ah, hombres. You need a refill."

"Sure," Slocum said. "Listen, was there a man named Gomez in here yesterday?"

"I know him. He was here, but he didn't stay long. You need him?"

"Where could we find him?" Slocum half rose and went for some money.

The man smiled. In a place were money was so short, the little whore had only charged the Kid fifty cents for a piece of ass. Money talked.

"You ever been to Loma Linda?"

Slocum had twenty dollars in his palm. The man nodded.

"How do I get there?" Slocum asked.

"I can draw you a map. Come over to the bar."

"Fill the mugs and I will go over there."

"*Sí*."

The man found a sale bill to write on. "You know he is a mean bastard?"

"That's why I want him."

"Here is Alto. Where you are is here. Take the right fork of the road going north and it will take you there."

"You know where he lives when he is there?"

"They say he has a brother named Guermo who has a business there. I have not been there in years."

"How far is it?"

"Two days' ride on a burro." The man smiled. "I never had a good horse to ride over there."

The man showed him two mountains to cross and some other points he recalled from the road there. Slocum realized the Madres were vast.

"Is there a church there?" he asked.

"Oh, *sí*, Saint Joseph."

"Good. I may need to pray there."

The big man crossed himself, Slocum guessed from just

thinking about it. "He has no army. He was jumpy when he came here. Does he know you are after him?"

"I think so. Here take this money, you need it."

"I feel like Judas telling you this for money."

"Gomez is not the Christ that Judas exposed."

"Oh, I know that. When he had his army, he would come here and demand to be waited on and rape men's wives in the village."

"What did he do yesterday?"

"Drank beer and looked glum. He never used a *puta*, nor was he interested in one. I think he was sick."

"Who rides with him?"

"A mean son of a bitch they call Goat. They say when he was a young he screwed them, because his cock was too big for the girls to let him use theirs."

"Is he dangerous?"

"Oh, *sí*. He did all the killing and bad things for Gomez."

"We will find him."

"Many people in the Madres will thank you. What happened to his army?"

"They all died in their sleep."

"Good place for them. I am glad to meet you, señor."

"The pleasure is mine." Then they shook hands.

The girl came back and slid into the booth beside the Kid. "He's gone to Loma Linda."

Slocum paid her a five-dollar gold piece. She beamed like he had paid her a fortune. They finished their beer and went back to camp loaded with the food supplies that Silva had asked for, including a slab of fresh-cut beef, sweet peppers, and onions. Slocum knew what she'd cook to please them.

She stood on her toes and kissed him for what he brought back.

"Tell me about the man they call Goat who rides with him," Slocum said.

"I was lucky I never felt his meanness. But he ripped women apart and strangled men who disobeyed him. They were making many raids then, and so he was off taking care of the army most of the time. I feared him more than any man who worked for Gomez, and there were more sons of bitches in that gang. I am glad they were blown up."

"The man at the Cantina told us that Gomez had done lots of bad things when he had his army in that village, but now he's acting defeated."

"Well he does not have all those men to do his bidding anymore. He knows you are coming. I told you that you would get him in the end."

He hugged her shoulder. "You are a wonderful woman. I am glad I borrowed you."

"So am I."

Charlie returned and told them that Gomez had taken the right fork in the road. Slocum thanked him for all his scouting and then told them what they had learned.

"People up here really hate him. He did some bad things in these places when he had his army."

"What is at Loma Linda?"

Slocum shook his head. "Some think his brother lives there."

"I have never been there."

With a nod, Slocum said, "Nor have we, but it is two days away on a burro."

They all laughed and fell into eating Silva's food.

Her presence had really helped Slocum with his men, and her food was the greatest thing. These men had been on lots of manhunts, but they had never eaten any better under such primitive conditions. They'd have done anything for her too. She was helped at every turn because of the effort she made for them.

Never in camp did she need anything—wood was there, water when she needed some; they even washed the dishes and helped her pack up to move. They knew about her hatred for what Gomez had done to her. She didn't complain or retell her past experience, but instead kept spirits up, including Slocum's. He felt she was an angel, and he admired her.

They loaded up for Loma Linda. The packhorses were ready. Silva stepped onto her horse, and, settled in the saddle, she thanked them for their help. Slocum sent Charlie ahead. They rode out and left the campsite behind. The morning air was still cool in the high mountains, a big change from the desert behind them. Silva wore a shawl over her shoulders and moved in close to Slocum.

"We could be on the last days of this business."

"You are an optimist," Slocum said and about laughed.

"A what?"

"Oh, someone who's convinced that they will win."

"Win, no—I will lose when you win. I can go back home to my children, my husband, my sister, and wash clothes at the village well. I don't mind that, but I know I won't win and be what you call it."

"Optimistic means you think well of life."

She nodded, but he knew he had not won her over.

The Sierra Madres were such a vast range of mountains. Slocum respected them. He and his group descended in a great valley and then climbed another range over twisty roads, until the fresh air swept their faces on the peak pass. The drudgery of the long journey showed on their faces, but Slocum also knew they were a united and tough small army.

Midday they had some tortilla-wrapped food Silva had packed for them, and they washed it down with tinny-tasting canteen water. The Kid stopped Silva. "If you did not have a family and husband, I would ask you to marry me."

She looked up at him. "And I would say yes 'cause you are a real man. You will find a woman you deserve. I have been flattered you asked me. I don't feel I ride for revenge, but I do. But being with all of you has been the finest adventure I ever have had, and I will never forget every moment. Thank you."

They mounted up again, then rode on across another mountain range and dropped into the next valley as the sun slipped down behind them. They made camp, and before the daylight was gone they hurried about to get her cook fire built and the horses unloaded.

The race, Slocum considered, ended as a tie. The sun went down and her fire lit the camp. She hurried about like usual, preparing food. Charlie and Gordon slipped out to learn what they could about Gomez's whereabouts and if they were close to him.

With fewer items to feed them, Silva apologized, but they told her not to worry, they knew how hard she had tried. Things were quiet under the million stars for a ceiling. A few red wolves howled, but they were distant. Charlie and Gordon returned and had word that Gomez was around, but his location was not clear. Both men ate late but thanked Silva. The fire's reflection gave off radiant heat as they all huddled under blankets for warmth.

"Summing up what we learned, we don't know much," Charlie said. "If he's here, he is hiding like a rat gone in a hole. I doubt he can raise an army here. My hunch is he has no money, and that was his strength before all this happened. It is the longest campaign I ever have had to resolve such a situation. I think we will find him. If not tomorrow, soon."

Slocum and Silva went to bed shortly after that. A guard shift had been set up. They were too close to Gomez not to have one. Under Slocum in the bedroll, she stretched out and sighed.

"Will you find him tomorrow?"

"I don't know."

"Then we can make love and forget him."

He kissed her and forgot him.

After breakfast they rode into the village. Ken and Silva stayed in camp to watch things. Slocum took on the large cantina. There were some gamblers playing cards. There were a few locals at the bar. This was a land of little money and few ways to make it.

The bartender brought him a bottle of mescal and a glass.

He spoke in Spanish. "You wish some mescal, señor?"

"I want far worse—an outlaw hiding here. A man who raped and robbed your neighbors. A worthless scoundrel hiding under someone's skirt in your village. He has killed innocent brave men without reason. I want this man. I will pay for finding him or I will pay for his head on a pike."

"Who is this hombre?"

"Raul Gomez. Does that make you uncomfortable that he is here?"

Some who had gathered to hear him nodded.

"Tell me where he is or bring his head on that pike."

"What about our families and homes?" one man asked.

"He will be dead. Ghosts won't hurt you."

They laughed.

One cardplayer tossed in his hand. "I am going home to be sure he is not there."

"May God go with you, sir."

No one else moved.

"His brother lives here. If he is part of his gang, I want him too."

No one spoke.

"Is there no one needs a hundred pesos?"

No reply.

"Oh, you are all rich and don't need any money?" He poured some liquor into his glass and shook his head. "My camp is west of this village. My money will spend."

He downed the contents. "When he rapes your daughter or wife, I won't cry for you, I will cry for them because you are such cowards."

The glass set back on the bar, his money for it beside the bottle, he still had no answer. He nodded to the bartender. "I thought real men lived in the Madres. I guess I was wrong."

At the door, a man shouted, "Let's help him find that *bastardo*. Manuel, you swore you'd kill him for what his men did to your daughter? Stand up."

The man did.

Slocum stopped inside the batwing doors. Another man stood up. "I will get my brothers. They will help. We will go with you and find him."

"He can't be far. Let us get him."

"Yes, we will help."

In the street Slocum sent the growing number of men in four directions. Gordon came up frowning and dismounted. "What the hell is going on?"

"These men are going looking for Gomez."

The big man frowned. "How the hell did you do that?"

"I challenged them in the cantina to find him for me. Many of their families have been hurt by him and his army in the past. I simply roused their anger."

"Sounds good. Do we wait?"

"We have to. If he is around here, they can find him."

Gordon hitched his horse. "I am willing to wait."

"Where are Charlie and the Kid?" Slocum asked him.

"I've not seen them since we got here."

"We better go look for them."

"Fine. Where?"

Slocum shook his head. "I have no idea. But we better be sure they are all right."

"I'll go west and you go east. This place isn't that big," Gordon said.

Slocum agreed and set out. He stopped two ladies. "I am looking for an Indian and a white boy. Have you seen them?"

"No, señor, but everyone is looking for that *bastardo* Gomez."

"I know. I sent them to find him."

The older woman, with her eyes set hard, said, "Let me have him when you catch him."

"Why?"

"I want to bash his balls one at a time with a mallet. He ruined my sister's life."

Slocum nodded. "We will find him."

"May God help you find him."

"Thanks."

He stopped an old man walking with a cane and asked him.

"No, everyone is looking for Gomez."

Where in the hell had they gone? He was becoming concerned, when a woman told him, "I saw them ride east an hour ago."

"Gracias." They must have a lead. Charlie was tough enough for the two of them, though the Kid had grown up a hell of a lot since they left Dan's place. Slocum still recalled his serious proposal to Silva. She was an impressive person, and he could see how the Kid had grown to admire her. This trip would have been a lot tougher without her and her food.

He started back to the cantina porch.

"Gomez must have fled," a man said. "We have looked everywhere."

"Well we tried," Slocum told the man. "Thanks." He hated to give up and let Gomez slip away again.

A group of men approached with a prisoner. They were hauling the haggard-looking man up the street. "This is his brother, Guermo. He did not know where his brother went, but he finally remembered."

"Where?"

"To Blanco Springs last night."

"How did you learn that?"

"We stuck a needle into his *huevos*. It helped his memory."

Slocum about shuddered over the notion of a needle in the balls. "Does Gomez have a horse?"

"*Sí*, he stole one. The horse he rode in on is near death."

"I appreciate all your help. I will set up a two-drink deal for everyone in the cantina. You are brave men." He went inside, and the bartender agreed for thirty dollars to give everyone two drinks. Slocum had no time to argue. He simply paid the bill and went out to get his horse.

Gordon arrived and reined in his horse. "They say he went to Blanco Springs," he said.

"I just learned that. They tortured his brother into telling them. I bought them all two drinks."

"Yeah, I spoke to the woman who loaned them the steel needle."

Slocum shook his head. "One way to get answers. I think Charlie and the Kid are on his tracks."

They galloped their horses and by midday overtook the two.

"You have his tracks?" Slocum asked Charlie.

"Sorry, we learned from some woman who hated him that he had stolen from her, and we hoped to have caught him by now."

Slocum nodded. "Lots of women hated him back there. I don't know why he even went there. Maybe his brother gave him some money. I think he was broke."

"Unless he was hiding it," the Kid said. "There were no signs of wealth at his last jacal. We found it, and his kids were in rags."

Charlie agreed. "He didn't even have a horse. He stole the one he rides."

"Maybe today we will catch him."

"The horse he stole has no shoes and its hooves are cracked. I told the Kid we'd have him in a few hours at the most."

"Good. We'll capture him."

Beside the road ahead sat a vaquero and a crippled horse. His head hung low, the animal looked to be in pain.

The man stood up and took his sombrero off to speak to them. "Some *tonto loco* hombre shot at me. Then he took my horse, my pistol, and my money. He is crazy. He said the devil was after him and a *bruja* told him he only had one life left to escape the devil's hand."

"Hell that must be us, men," Slocum said, and they all laughed. "Climb on behind the Kid. We will find you another horse or get yours back. What is your name?"

"Cruz."

Slocum introduced the others and they set out again.

"You know who he was?" the Kid asked Cruz.

"No."

"That was the big outlaw Raul Gomez."

"I am lucky to be alive," Cruz said and crossed himself.

"Yeah, he's pretty desperate. He had a helper when we started after him this time, but he even cut out. I don't guess we even know his name, do we, Slocum?"

"No, he vanished like thin air. I'd almost forgotten him. They called him Goat."

"When Gomez had no money, he must have jumped ship," Gordon said and spurred his horse to keep up.

It was near sundown in the deep canyon when they approached the village. The bell was ringing in the tower over the small church.

When they came in the village gate, Cruz shouted, "There is my horse and saddle, thank God."

Slocum drew his gun and stepped down, checking the growing shadows for any sign of the thief. A window was broken, and a shot was fired from a shop.

In the confusion of their panicked horses, Slocum returned fire. Then the blinding dust the horses had made boiled up, and a voice shouted, "Hold your fire or she dies."

A desperate-faced man came out on the shop porch with a hostage. He pointed a cocked pistol at a pretty teenage girl's head and used her for a shield. Her face was ash-white and her eyes wide open. No doubt the man's grip on a handful of her long hair hurt, but the shock of this happening to her was worse.

"Drop you guns in the dirt and back away."

"Do it, men," Slocum said. The muscle under his right eye was twitching. They had to obey this madman until an opening showed. There might not be one, but they'd still run him down afterward.

He was slipping around them with the girl still held by the hair and the gun ready, to get around to Slocum's horse.

Slocum wanted the Spencer in the scabbard, but there was too much space between him and the horse. Gomez could shoot him twice if he moved for it.

"Get in the saddle," he ordered the girl, still covering them with his pistol.

With the girl on the horse, Gomez stepped into the stirrup and had his back exposed for a split second. Enough time for a flying Bowie knife that struck him hard and stayed in him. Gomez screamed then fell backward on the ground.

"Nice throw," Slocum said to the Kid.

He looked to be in shock. "I only stuck it in a tree once. That makes the second time. Whew."

Gordon took the knife out of him, but Gomez was gurgling in death.

"You used your last life, you dumb bastard," Gordon said, standing over him.

The Kid held his arms out and caught the girl getting off the horse. She gratefully poured kisses on his face as he held her in his arms off the ground. He kissed her back.

Charlie was squatted in the dust, looking at the dying outlaw. "Where is all the gold and silver you stole?"

"In the—casa—" He died.

"Did you hear him?" Charlie asked, closing Gomez's eyelids.

Slocum nodded. "I bet they've found it by now, but we can go back and look."

"Sure, why not?" Gordon said. "I didn't think it would end like this. If the dumb bastard had gone on, he might have lived, but like that witch told him, he only had one life left."

"Many don't listen to such advice." Slocum looked around for him. "The Kid is the real hero. Where did they go?"

Gordon put his hand on Slocum's shoulder. "I think those two had business to tend to. Come on, Cruz, the boss is buying the booze when we get these horses hitched."

"Good. This has been a helluva day for me. First I am robbed, my horse taken, then I am in a crazy shoot-out."

A priest appeared, having heard the commotion and come to see to the dying man.

"Here, Father, are ten pesos to bury him." Slocum paid the man in robes, who gratefully accepted it. "I would not bury him inside the church cemetery. He was a man of many bad deeds."

Two of the priest's helpers carried the body off. The padre never said yes or no to Slocum's request.

Slocum herded his three inside the cantina and ordered a bottle of good mescal and glasses. Silva and Ken would be worried, but they'd tell them the story of Gomez's demise when they got back the next day. He also ordered food for them.

"Señor," the bartender said, "I can have some boys put up your horses for the night. No one will steal anything."

"Give them a peso apiece and have them handle it," Slocum said.

"Very generous, señor. Your food is being cooked. There will be pallets to sleep on as well tonight, or you may sleep free with one of the ladies that work here."

Cruz raised his hand. "I accept."

"Good." The bartender laughed. "We appreciate all of you. That man was a vicious person for many years in these mountains. Good he is dead tonight."

They were wined and dined that evening. Slocum slept by himself despite many generous offers from the women in the village. Silva had spoiled him too much to even try finding a match for her skills in bed. But he slept easier.

Haggard and looking worn out, the Kid joined them when they saddled up in the morning.

"Hey thanks," Gordon told him. "We couldn't have done it without you."

"Yeah—second time it stuck in something. Man, I knew it was throw it right or die. Instead I died last night in her arms. If I fall off my horse today, reload me belly-down. I want some more of Silva's good food."

They teased him all day about his night in the arms of his love. He simply smiled and shook his head. "I didn't think you could get a headache from having too much sex."

In Loma Linda, the curious came to hear about the outlaw's fate. Slocum turned it over to the Kid to tell them, while he went and found a butcher who had beef. He also bought onions along with sweet peppers and wine before they headed back to their camp.

With her skirt in hand, Silva ran out to greet them. "You finally got him?"

Slocum stepped down and hugged her. "The Kid got him. We helped."

"It wasn't no big deal." The Kid took the reins of Slocum's horse. "I'll put him up. But we brought the fixings for supper. We've been eating hog slop, I tell you."

"I knew you hombres would miss me." She stood on her toes and kissed Slocum. "I missed you too."

"It was a long night." He chuckled and hugged her.

"We were concerned."

"He told us, dying, that his gold and silver were in his casa."

"Oh, what do you think?"

"Someone may have found it already, but we'll go back and look for it."

"I have to get cooking. The food must have been bad— the Kid eats anything."

They both laughed.

"Will we go back tomorrow?"

"We may have to shoe some of our horses. But the next day we will head that way."

"Good. I have you for another week."

"Yes."

She smiled and ran for her "kitchen."

"We'll need four horses shod," Gordon said.

"Let's take them to town. You and I can help the black-smith and get it done. Ken, the Kid, and Charlie can go over saddle girths and pack saddles and be ready to go back."

"We can do that."

"Then we shall. I know you're anxious to get home to Alma."

"It has been a long deal, but she will understand."

"You are a lucky man to have such a woman who respects you, and you respect her."

"We have a great life. A good farm and water for it; I have enjoyed the crops."

"Well I want to look for any fortune that Gomez might have left. I thank you for helping me. Dan will pay all of you for your time."

"Whenever you need help, come find me."

"I will."

"Good."

That all settled, Slocum checked on Silva as the sun set.

"We will have supper in a short while," she said, patting out another flour tortilla.

"I know. We can wait. Just checking." He dropped down and sat cross-legged on the ground.

"Did you ever think of settling someplace?" she asked, busy working on her project.

"Aw, my soles would itch. There are things in my past that never could be ironed out, and hired men would come for me. No, I will keep moving, I guess, till I drop."

"You ever need to hide out, come by St. Barnabas. I would go with you somewhere and hide out with you."

"Thanks. I know *I* would enjoy it anyway."

She rose up on her knees and put the freshly made tortilla on the grill to cook. Then she began to form another. "It has been lots of work. But I have enjoyed myself and all of you."

"I bet you never thought when you told me you'd help me it would end this way."

"No. A poor Mexican woman was scrubbing clothes and needed a break, and why not do it with a tall gringo hombre? Plus I hated Gomez and his man for my own treatment."

He nodded.

"So, in a few days, I can go back and be a wife and mother again."

"None of us will forget you."

She shook her head and dismissed his words.

After supper they made love and slept tight in each other's arms. Before dawn they woke, made love again, and she slipped out of bed to start food.

After the meal, Slocum and Gordon rode out for town leading the horses that needed shoes. The blacksmith agreed to work with them. He had some used shoes that would have to work since he had no supply of new ones. Two horses had good enough shoes to reset. Slocum was pleased that they'd be shod anyway.

The three men worked hard and by midday had the old iron shoes pulled off and hooves trimmed and shaped. Slocum paid the blacksmith five pesos for his part, and it was probably more than he made in a week or more.

They rode back, and he and Silva slipped off to bathe in a cold stream. It was a leisurely afternoon. In the morning they'd ride back to the hacienda. The notion that Gomez's treasure might still be there made Slocum interested in searching the casa ruins. Then he would return to Patagonia.

He wondered if Saundra was back teaching school. He'd have to see.

10

The pack train was following the riders. The kid was in charge of the four packhorses for the day. He'd been in high spirits with the outfit.

"I'm going back to herd cows, lady and gentlemen. And I think I am ready."

"It will be hard for you to adjust," Gordon said over his shoulder as they rode under the pines.

"It damn sure will. I have had a great time with you, Gordon."

"Me too."

Up front, Slocum nodded and twisted in the saddle. "Don't let your guard down. Gomez still may have leftover people that want to resurrect his power."

Everyone nodded. They came off the mountain range in a long day's push and were glad to reach the campground. The small street markets were already closed, so Silva cooked beans and turned up her hands. "Nothing more I can do."

They laughed and applauded.

The Kid was concerned about a packhorse's hoof that must have been bruised on the trail. He stood the brown horse in the creek, hoping the cool water might get the swelling and pain down while they ate.

Afterward, Slocum and the Kid went back to check on the horse. When they led him out of the water, he still was gimpy on the leg.

"We may need to replace him tomorrow if we can find another," Slocum said.

"I ain't being a baby about things. That horse came from Dan's. I rode him a lot. Maybe he can make it back and heal. I don't want to leave him in Mexico."

"He can make it back, we'll take him. I understand your feeling for him. We left enough horses at the first camp— maybe we can make it back with this one."

"Good. That makes me feel better."

Slocum clapped him on the shoulder. "You did your share, and I'd ride the river with you anytime."

The Kid dropped his chin. "I guess you know that makes me feel real good. I wondered about this big guy who came to Dan's and was going to wipe out that outlaw. I am proud I rode with all of you. I won't forget it."

"Neither will I."

They went to bed, Slocum with his sweet companion.

"Are you tired?" she asked.

"Sure. It was a long day. You tired?"

"Not tired enough to miss you stirring me up."

He kissed her and they made love.

At dawn they saddled, packed, and rode off. The brown horse carried empty packs and kept up. Slocum felt a little stiff and blank as they rode in the growing heat of the day. They were out of the cooler air, and the dusty, dry sun-heated land stretched for miles ahead.

That night out of habit Slocum asked the men to take turns standing guard. Each man drew a shift, and he went to bed with Silva.

The two of them were talking and savoring the chance to lie down together, skin to skin.

"I think Juan Romales was killed before you came. There was also Pasco. He was another mean *bastardo* in the Gomez ranks. No one spoke of him, did they?"

"No one up there ever mentioned anyone," he said.

"Oh," she said, acting ready to hug and kiss him. "There will always be some more to take their place. Love me."

Later, Charlie woke him with a hand over his mouth. "We have company."

Slocum nodded and put his finger to her lips. He moved out from the blanket with his britches up. He had his six-gun in his fist, trying to locate any movement or sounds. Charlie quietly woke the others.

They were soon all awake and armed, keeping low in the starlight. Slocum heard a strange horse and nodded. This horse was communicating with theirs horses—that's how Slocum knew it was an outsider. Someone coughed beyond the camp. The hair on Slocum's neck rose when someone ran over the gravel under the hill.

He dried his hand on his pants and recovered the Colt. They were out there. Would they wait till dawn, when they would be able to see their targets? Night insects still chirped. There was hardly a rim of light on the horizon to the east. He could smell the oil on his gun and the burnt smell of spent gunpowder.

Then someone shouted, "Take them!"

Men wearing sombreros emerged in sight, firing pistols like wild men and charging them. A deadly array of shots cut the strangers down, and there was silence, save for the cries of the wounded. A cloud of eye-burning smoke hung in the air. With caution Slocum and his men rose.

"None of us are hurt," Gordon said.

"Good," Slocum said. "Disarm them. Make sure they are comfortable. When it is settled, send someone for medical aid. Silva will make a meal and we will ride. How many men were out there?" he asked Charlie.

"A dozen maybe."

"I thought so. It's over, Silva," he said to her.

She came out from under the covers—dressed. "Good, I never heard so many shots around me in my life."

"Charlie, we need to learn the leader's name too."

"We can do that."

"Our horses are all here and fine," the Kid reported. "We can take theirs with us. The good ones, I mean."

"Good idea," Slocum said and smiled. The Kid had really grown up.

Charlie returned as Slocum helped stoke Silva's cooking fires.

"The man who hired them was called Pasco."

Silva exchanged a look of I-told-you-so with Slocum. They continued to work on the food preparation. When it was done, Gordon and Ken arrived to dump armloads of weapons on the ground. Silva served them tortillas wrapped around a sugary dry apple/raisin combination that they smiled over.

The Kid held his up. "Bandits raid us and she still comes through with desert. Hurrah for Silva."

They agreed.

"How about the raiders?" Slocum asked Charlie.

"Five are dead."

Ken nodded. "A few more will die, and some will survive with medical care."

"Where did Pasco go?"

"He rode away, they said."

"Did anyone see him to know his face?"

"I saw his horse," Charlie said. "He was a big black stallion."

"Beware of the dark horse," Slocum said. Damn—cut the head off one snake, and another slithers out.

Packhorses were loaded and saddled, and they rode out, herding the rest and not looking back. This could be their last day on the road. Slocum planned to go to the casa site and search for any overlooked treasure. In late afternoon they arrived at the burned-out shell of the place, and the fire smell was still there.

"There is a safe no one has opened down here," Ken said, leading the way. "It has been beat to death and not opened."

"Reckon anything is left in it?" Slocum asked.

"I don't know much about safes. They tried to blow it up. They beat it to death with axes and sledgehammers." Ken stood, pushed his hat back on his head, and looked awfully skeptical.

"We can tie some blasting sticks on the hinges and blow them up," Slocum said.

"Wait, wait," the Kid hollered, running over. "Anyone listened to the dial?"

"I don't think you can turn it," Slocum said.

On his knees, the Kid studied the battered remains of a dial. His ear to the side, he listened for any sound.

"It still turns."

"You hear anything?" Ken asked

"Maybe a click. I'm going back."

Some bird went to making a yakking sound. The kid was trying to get his ear closer to hear the works inside. He said, "Shoot that bird."

Slocum looked around for it. No one could see the bird.

Everyone squatted around the Kid as he fidgeted with the dial. Time went by, and he kept trying to figure the right dial turns by clicks. The temperature rose, and someone went for water.

Slocum stepped up. "Have you tried to open it?"

"The handle is broke off."

"There is a hole in that knob on the left. Let's find an iron rod to go in there and try to open it."

Ken and Gordon got to their feet. The Kid kept listening and twisting.

In the fire's ashes, Ken found a rod about the size of the hole.

The Kid stood up, took the rod, inserted it, and first it bent on him, but then it began to twist. He gave up and almost smiled. "Now it is so messed up, it'll never open."

He kicked the door with his heel in anger, and the door fell off. His reward was all the tarnished coins that spilled out. Not ten or twenty, but a wealth of them.

"How much is there?" Ken asked, looking at the shifting coins.

"The canvas sacks burned up in there, and so did the folding money." Slocum straightened up. "Thanks, Kid, but I'd say all us working together opened it, so everyone get a canvas bucket and we will divide it. As they say, 'To the victor go the spoils.'

"Silva, you as a shareholder get a bucket," he told her as she stood frozen in place, in shock over the amount of money before them.

"Here's you a bucket." The Kid handed her one.

"Where did all the buckets come from?" she asked.

Gordon shook his head. "They were in an out building."

Charlie was putting handfuls of all denominations in the buckets. The Kid went in and helped him spread the wealth. In the end there were five buckets near full of an array of coins.

"Where's your pail?" Gordon asked Slocum.

"She gets mine."

The Kid scoffed. "That ain't fair."

"It suits me. Now we need to sew canvas bags to carry it back home."

"Hell, it would take packhorses to carry it," the Kid said.

"It will. Maybe two. But we have plenty of horses," Slocum reminded him. "Let's put our find in our camp. Two men to guard it. The rest of us will see if we can find this outlaw Pasco."

"How bad can he be?" Gordon asked.

"He won't surrender to us. But if he's around someplace, we can get him," Slocum said. "Let's go find him."

"Where do we look for him?"

"Try the cantinas. Someone will know. Who guards the money?"

Ken said he and the Kid would watch it. The others nodded in agreement.

"You know, if he comes around and knows you have it, there will be hell to pay," Slocum said.

"We'll be ready," Ken said.

The other two rode out, leaving Silva with Slocum. He needed to take her back to her village, and he hated to part with her. They first needed to find this outlaw.

Charlie spotted Pasco's black horse at a hitch rack. Salt coated his legs and chest; the devil must have run him for miles.

"That's his horse," Charlie said. "You won't miss him. He's a big guy. I'll guard the back door."

Slocum agreed. He dismounted and went alongside the deep-breathing black and loosened the cinch. With another look around, he headed through the batwing doors.

After a second to let his eyes adjust to the darker room, he went to the bar and ordered a bottle of mescal with two glasses. He hadn't seen the big man. But several were off to the side under a lamp, no doubt gambling. Gordon joined him at the bar. Slocum poured them out some mescal in the glasses.

"It is three dollars for the bottle, señor," the bartender said.

"Sure, we buy them all the time. You know a bandit son of a bitch named Pasco?" He slapped the money on the bar.

"I think we found him," Gordon said with his hand on his gun.

Some cardplayer fell over backward to clear the line of sight from Slocum to the man under the sombrero fixing to get out of his chair.

"Who the hell are you?" the Mexican asked.

"Did you send a half dozen men to raid my camp?"

"So I did. What are you going to do about it?"

"Get your hand away from that gun butt or you will be where we sent those dumb peons you sent to kill me and my compadres."

"Who are you?"

"Slocum's my name, Pasco. He's Gordon. Now we've met you, put your hands in the air."

"What will you do with me?"

"Parade you up and down the street and ask women if you raped them or their daughters."

"You can't do that to me."

"Why not?"

"They would kill me."

"That's the idea. Your reign of terror is over. Stand easy. Gordon, get his gun. Hands a little higher. That's good."

Gordon disarmed him and shoved him toward the door. "You're lucky. We kill birds like you. This way you can tell them in hell you faced a mob to get there."

They shoved him outside the cantina in the bright

daylight. Slocum fired two shots in the air to get people's attention.

In Spanish, Gordon invited them all to come over there. Folks ran to hear what he would say and who the big man was standing up there like their prisoner.

"This is the outlaw Pasco. Five days ago, my posse killed his boss, Raul Gomez, in the Madres. He is gone. His men were killed in the barracks explosions. One last thread of that man is here. They raped and robbed all you people. He was the man in charge. Should we turn him lose to screw your wives and steal the little money you have, or will you all be men and put him in a grave where he deserves to be?"

"In the grave!" they began to shout.

"Do you need a pistol?"

"No," a woman said. "We have guns. Can we have his gun?"

"Sure." Gordon hoisted it out of his waistband and gave it to her.

Two-handed, she cocked the hammer and raised the pistol to shoot the outlaw.

"Do you remember me?"

He shook his head.

"You ruined my life back then. Today is my day. I am going to ruin yours."

The gun roared. Pasco grabbed his chest. She shot again. He was sprawled on his back pleading.

"I cried and you never stopped."

She shot him in the face, and then her two-handed grip on the gun failed and she dropped to her knees, crying and praying, "Father, forgive me for I have sinned. Hail Mary—"

Other women came to hug and comfort her.

Slocum waved his arm to get their attention. "Remember this day, *amigos*. A woman has shown she can kill a coward and a bully."

Charlie had joined them. He nodded to Slocum, and they rode back to camp.

Silva came out to meet them.

"You all look so glum. What is wrong?"

"Nothing," Slocum said. "I bought some canvas, large needles, and heavy thread to make coin sacks. Silva, show them how to make them."

"Where is Pasco?" she asked.

"He's dead. The reign of Gomez is over."

Dismounted, he stood by his horse. She handed the canvas and items to Gordon. "Hold these," she said.

Then she ran around and hugged Slocum. "Why are you so sad? Those bastards you came for are all dead. You found every one of us lots of money. What is wrong?"

He kissed her cheek and whispered, "And now I must lose you."

"Not till in the morning."

"Good."

They went off the next day, and she rode one of the spare horses.

When they arrived at the well in the village, Silva's sister was doing wash and ran over with her wet dress showing her boobs and navel through the wet material. The two women hugged and danced. Slocum dismounted.

"You met my sister," Silva said. "Like I said, she's been taking care of things here. You kiss her good for me."

Her sister was not as slender as Silva, but she had a nice body and they kissed long.

In a low voice, he asked Silva if her sister knew about the reward. She wrinkled her nose. "Kiss him again," she said to her sister, "and I will tell you why later."

So her sister did, and then Slocum mounted up and rode away on his pacing horse to catch the others headed home.

In Nogales they sold their extra horses and he gave the money to the four men, who tried to give him some of it.

He refused it, and they went on to Dan's place and had a party.

Slocum learned that the Apache scare was over when he and Dan talked.

"What do I owe you and your men?" Dan asked.

"Me you owe two fifty, the men a hundred apiece, and that will square the three of us. Your men as well as mine have some money they recovered. But they earned that. Gomez is no more, and his gang are sprouting weeds."

"Oh, I owe you more than two hundred fifty."

"That's all I need."

"I'll get the money out of the safe and pay you three. But my cook will expect you to entertain her."

They both laughed.

"I can do that," Slocum said. "I'm in no hurry. Though I think Gordon and Charlie want to go on home."

"I'll get that money."

Slocum gathered the crew. "Dan's gone for your money. He's paying you two a hundred apiece and I will get two fifty."

"You should get a thousand," the Kid said.

"No, all I need are some expenses. I want to tell you how much I appreciate all four of you. Silva is back home, and we know she is rich by her standards. She will be fine. All those bastards are dead. We can ride on and live our lives."

"I ain't the speaker for everyone, but I won't ever forget it," the Kid said. "You ever need me, I want to go with you."

"The same here," Ken said.

"I live in St. David," Gordon told them all. "You are welcome at my house."

Charlie Horse stood and shrugged. "I used to live in a

wickiup, but we will have a jacal after this and a garden. Come stay with me."

"And any of you need anything, come see me," Dan said, handing out the money to them.

Slocum kissed Goldie good-bye and promised to return. She threatened him with her finger and said, "You better."

Then he hopped on the pacing horse that Dan had given him and headed for Patagonia.

There was a note for him at the hotel desk.

> *Dear Slocum,*
>
> *I have gone back to my schoolhouse. They sent a driver for me. I am somewhat lost without you, but I understand. Our affair has given me more backbone. After the school session I may go back to Kansas and live my life up there. I know now I can be a real woman, and you gave me the strength to see that.*
>
> *God bless you.*
> *Sandy*

Slocum looked at the letter and nodded.

"Anything I can do for you, sir?" the desk clerk asked. "She was a very lovely lady."

"She was that. You hit the nail on the head."

Slocum turned and left the hotel. Sandy didn't need him anymore. She'd find her way all right without him meddling in her life. He felt stiff and numb from the Mexican expedition. What he needed was a place to put up his boots and get settled back.

A woman with her face full of tears came across the street to meet him. "Wait. Wait."

"What can I do for you?"

She sniffed, and tears ran down her face. "They killed him. You knew Earl Reed my husband."

"Yes. You have a ranch up in the Mule Shoe Mountains. I knew Earl. Who killed him?"

"I don't know. He's dead. They said they buried him. I am stuck here and I have two small children. I don't know what I can do. I saw you, and you are the first person that I even knew in days. I am about to collapse."

He hugged her. "Why can't you go back?"

"One of my horses died of colic after we got here." She turned up her hands. "I have no money. There was some money at the ranch. Earl said he had to stay there and protect it."

"You had any food lately?"

"No."

"Get those two kids and let's go eat."

She looked taken back. "I am not begging."

"I am. Let's go to lunch, I need some. Where are they?"

"I'll get them. I can repay you—"

"Quit worrying. You need to eat."

She took him across the street to their wagon, and two small children there acted bashful.

"This is Harry, he's five. He's my big man."

Slocum kneeled down and spoke to him. "Harry, you doing all right?"

He nodded, rather reserved. "You made Mother stop crying, didn't you?"

"I tried." Harry ran over and hugged him.

His three-year-old sister, Lena, came behind him, not to be left out. One in each arm Slocum carried them across the street.

They had lunch in the café, and the kids were friendly to him.

Slocum said, "I have some friends at St. David who will care for them. Then we can go see about things at the ranch."

"I don't want to be a burden to you. I'm just—"

"We're going to get it all straight. I'll find a horse to match your other one. Then we can park the kids, go up there, and straighten things out. I have nothing else I need to do right now, so I am your helper."

"My savior. Thank you. I have been at a loss to do anything."

"No, I'm just a friend. Your name is?"

"Jena. I am sorry. I was so upset I have considered some crazy things to get out of here."

"Slocum is mine."

She nodded. "I have lost some of my senses. I knew your name when I saw you."

"Let's take the children up to my friends Gordon and Alma Morales at St. David. They have no children and will treat them well. Then we can go down and see about your ranch."

"But I have no horse."

"That is going to be cured in an hour. I'm going to hire some teenage boys to help you load it. By dark or tomorrow we will be up at St. David."

He paid for their lunch and told Jena to go back to the wagon and start loading.

"I'll try," she said, shaking her head.

"Work those boys I send you."

She agreed, and he kissed Lena as he set her down. "Harry, you help her too. I'll be back."

He found two boys loafing around at the livery. "There is a wagon up on Main Street needs two loaders. Mrs. Reed wants to go home. I'll pay you a dollar apiece to go help her do that. Her name is Jena Reed."

After sending them to help her, he found a decent team

and harness and bought them for a hundred dollars. He drove them down to Jena's wagon.

Her face was flushed, but she and the boys about had the wagon loaded. "We're near ready."

He handed her a towel to wipe her wet face. "You were working too hard. Get up on the wagon. You must try this team and see if you can handle them. I'll hand you the kids."

"Are you hooking them up?"

"No. The boys can hook them up."

They were soon ready, with everyone on board, including the calico cat named Susie.

Slocum stood in the front of the covered wagon, and the boys brought him the lines. Quietly, he spoke to the horses. They danced a little, but he clucked to them and they went forward slow-like, feeling the load. Then he swung them around and they acted fine. He halted them and gave Jena the reins.

He climbed down. "Jena, drive them out. I'll ride my horse and lead your extra one."

She agreed and took the reins. He quickly decided she could drive the team. There was lots of tomboy in her. That evening they made camp short of St. David because of the darkness. The tired children in a bedroll, the two adults sat cross-legged on the ground at the small fire and talked.

"I am in your debt, Slocum. I was so desperate without a horse and trapped there. I know he's dead, but how and why I may never know."

"Did they say anything?"

"Yes. 'Mrs. Reed, we buried your husband two days ago.' He was a polite cowboy, but I didn't get his name. I had seen him before, but I couldn't recall the name."

"Nothing we can do about it now. Gordon and Alma can babysit the kids until we make some sense of this. They are fine people."

"That might be best."

"It will be."

"Can I impose on you some more?"

"How so?"

"Could I sit on your lap?"

"Heavens yes."

"I feel so shaky, my skin is crawling."

He went and found a chair in the wagon and set it up. She used her hands to brush off any clinging grass or sticks on her rump. She was light on his legs and he hugged her tight. "We'll get it all straight."

Her shoulders shook and he hugged her tight. She turned and he softly kissed her. That was a spark, and they soon were getting worked up.

He whispered, "I am not here to take advantage of you."

"No. No. I need it. Can we go to your bedroll?"

"Only if you are sure."

"I'm not sure of much, but I am spoiled. Earl and I had a great marriage. I know he is gone but—"

His mouth closed on hers and she hugged his neck. He carried her to the bedroll, and they undressed under the stars. He went easy, letting her lead, and by the time they were coupled she was on fire. A wiry, muscled, slender woman, she had a fiery spirit in sex, and in the end she near fainted.

They slept until before dawn, then had a short session before leaving the bedroll. When they finished, she swept the hair from her face and smiled. "I'm better."

When they drove in, Alma met them in the yard and had to pick up both children when she learned their purpose. The children had Alma stop for Susie to follow them. In a few hours, Jena was satisfied Harry and Lena could stay there and be happy. After lunch, when Gordon came in and met everyone, he was as proud as Alma at having the children in their care.

Slocum and Jena left for her place. They passed through bustling Tombstone and by sundown reached her ranch. She found the front door of the house broken down. The inside was a mess of scattered flour and rampaging. With a candle lamp she surveyed the damage while Slocum put up the horses. He saw the grave they'd marked with a crude cross. There would be few answers for her questions about what happened. Would she stay there? There were not many choices for a woman with two children. Slocum left the four horses in a trap with water and went to the house.

"Oh, you must be hungry," she said. "I don't see much that can't be cleaned up and fixed. They didn't burn the place down. I don't know if I am lucky or what."

"Can I make a fire?"

"Yes, when the weather was like this, I cooked in that open building."

"What do you think?"

"I have some oatmeal I can boil."

"That sounds all right."

"Slocum, should I sell this place or try to find a few hands and run it?"

He held her around the waist and swung her back and forth as the fire in the sheet-metal cooking range began to catch. "If you think you can stand it, I'd ranch. We can find a couple of cowboys, and you have cows and calves to sell. The beef market at Tombstone will help you. The army will have to settle the Apaches. But you have no trade like being a seamstress, and you don't want to cook for a café. This ranch should raise your children."

"Let me put the water on for the oatmeal."

They sat together on a bench by the range and talked more about her future. They kissed and she smiled. "I am getting myself back in gear. I miss him and will, but I need to get my life on too. You said I was not a seamstress. That is not an exaggeration. Don't rip your clothes, I can't fix them."

They kissed as the sun went down. In a short while they ate her oatmeal and he went for his bedroll. "We can sleep in it."

"Sounds lovely."

He spread it out on the floor inside. They undressed and, naked, went under the first cover. They were soon in each other's arms, and she cried some.

"It's not you. I had such a serious life. A great husband, two children, and a growing ranch. My house was nice and not white with flour and turned upside down." She sniffed. "Love me and maybe I can forget."

They made soft, quiet love in his bedroll, and when they were through, she whispered, "You are a wonderful treatment for an insane woman."

"You're great to treat."

The next day he caught two horses and saddled one for her. They rode part of the range looking at her longhorn-shorthorn cross cows and their roan calves. They found a few of their shorthorn bulls that stood up and stretched their backs, while the spookier longhorn cross cows and calves left when they rode in.

"You have some great cattle," he said to her.

"Earl was a good cattleman."

"I think you can hire some men and make this ranch business work."

"Could you stay for a while and get things settled here?"

"Sure. But you never know when I may have to leave."

"I knew you have troubles from your past. But I want this place set up so I can operate it."

"We will need a bunkhouse built for your crew. I can go down on the border and get a building crew. Do you have any money?"

"No. Earl handled all that. They never mentioned finding any money on him. Surely they would not have buried it with him."

"He keep it somewhere?"

"In a coffee can. I never saw it in that messy house."

"Let's ride back and look for it."

Back at the ranch they searched the house for the can. It was nowhere in sight. They sat down and shook their heads. It was gone.

"In his last hours, knowing his fate, he may have hid it."

"Where?"

"Jena, I don't know this ranch like you do."

"Let's search the saddle shed. Why didn't they burn the buildings?"

"I don't know. They burned most of these places they raided."

"There is no sign they even tried."

They found cans of horseshoe nails and bits, harness hardware, and some saddle pads, plus three saddles untouched by the raiders. There was no coffee can with money in it.

Outside, Jena leaned with her butt to the wall, and Slocum squatted on the ground. "No money anywhere."

"No, but why they didn't take all this or scatter it is beyond me."

"Would you know the man who told you they buried him?"

"I think I have seen him before. I would know him if I saw him again."

"We need more information on Earl's death. He is the only man who knows how he was killed."

The next day they started checking on other ranchers in the area. At the Jeb Douglas Ranch, Jeb told them how he learned about Earl's death.

Jeb said, "Shorty Branch told me at the cantina that they found him facedown. Never said much else. We speculated it was the Apaches done it."

"Who else spoke about it?" Slocum asked him.

"Why're you digging this up?"

"She and I don't think Apaches killed him. But we never saw his wounds. They never stole anything but money. Just scattered flour all over hell."

Jeb scratched his ear hard. "Why do that?"

"Someone wanted his ranch bad enough to kill him?"

"By God, you think he was murdered for his ranch?"

"I don't think anything. I just want questions answered. Her husband is dead. The killers never stole his horses. They were in the trap. Does that sound like Apaches?"

"By God no."

"Someone did steal the coffee can that had our money in it," Jena added.

Jeb frowned. "You going over and see if Behan will come arrest him?"

"We don't have any proof who it is. Besides, Behan hardly gets out of Tombstone."

"I know that, but damn, it does sound funny blaming Apaches when they more than likely didn't do it."

"We've got more checking to do." Slocum made a head toss toward their horses.

"Keep you ears open, Jeb," Jena said. "Thanks."

"I will, Jena. I sure will."

They talked to two more small ranchers and didn't get back until after dark. When they dropped off their horses at the saddle shed, Slocum slipped around and cut Jena off from speaking with his hand over her mouth.

In her ear, he whispered, "Company."

Her eyes grew wide, and he pointed for her to stay there between the two horses. Grasshoppers were chirping in the night, along with crickets. He tried to make soft steps as he headed for the house. No one in sight, but a strange horse nicker had alerted him that there was someone there.

At the door, he stood aside, pulled the latch string, and the door fell open inward. Three shots from inside broke the night's silence. Then someone went to coughing on the gun smoke and staggered to the door all bent over. Slocum coldcocked him with his pistol butt.

He grunted and that was cut short.

"You all right?" Jena asked, sounding shaken.

"I'm fine, Jena. You can come now." He bent over and disarmed the intruder of a knife and his gun. "Light a lamp and we'll see if you know him."

The man was groggy when Slocum jerked him up by the collar and hauled him inside the cabin. "What's your name?"

The man didn't answer.

Jena lighted a candle lamp. "I never saw him before. He's Mexican."

"Get some rope. He'll talk to us in a short while. His memory will get better."

"I have some," she said and went to a trunk for it.

Slocum bound the Mexican's hands behind his back and the back of the chair, then tied his ankles to the chair legs.

"Tell us your name?"

Stone-faced, he never said a word.

"Heat some water," Slocum told Jena. "He'll find his tongue."

"I'll make us some supper too."

"Good."

"He would have shot us when you opened the door, wouldn't he?"

"He's a sorry hired pistolero. I heard a strange horse nicker at ours when we rode up. He wasn't in the trap, so there had to be someone here. I just stumbled on the notion that he was inside."

"Did he kill Earl?"

"He will talk in a little while."

"How are you so sure? He's like a cigar store Indian sitting here."

"When we pour boiling water down his throat, he'll talk."

"You savvy boiling water?" She had stuck in his face a large knife to slice off salt pork.

"I did nothing."

"No, you just tried to shoot him." She put the edge of the knife on the tip of his nose. "Did you shoot my husband?"

"No."

"Who hired you?"

He shook his head. "No one."

"You better tell me."

His arms folded on his chest, Slocum said, "I bet the horse he rode in on has a brand on him."

The man closed his eyes and shook his head in defeat. "Sherman Riddle."

"Sherman? You must be lying. He owns the wagon wheel brand."

"He hired me."

She stopped and squeezed her chin. "Come to think of it, that same cowboy who told me that they had buried Earl,

I saw him at roundup. Never thought no more about that. I knew his face was familiar, but I was so wrought-up over the news I must have lost my mind and forgot it all."

"Be calm, Jena. I want you to go in the morning and gather folks that we talked to today. Tell them to get some more honest people, and we will take José here and call Riddle out."

She shook her head. "There isn't any law here to do this?"

"I wouldn't trust them. I don't know Riddle, but I bet he'd hire a fancy lawyer and get away with it."

"Then by God I'll do it. Let's eat. We'll have plenty to do then."

She hurried about making supper. When it was done, they sat down and ate. They had some biscuits and gravy left, with some fried potatoes. Slocum untied the man, set his pistol on the table, and told him to eat fast. After the meal, he took him to the saddle shed, tied him up good, and tossed him a saddle pad for a blanket.

"I will freeze."

"Naw, you'll be fine," Slocum said, and going out, he locked the door with a padlock Jena had given him.

In bed, she was shaking in his arms. "Why did he want this ranch? I never trusted or liked the way he looked at me from time to time. Earl said he didn't know any better than that. But to have shot Earl and then buried him like the Apaches did it is bad."

Slocum kissed her hard and raised her nightgown.

"Oh hell. I don't need to wear anything in bed with you. It will get in our way, huh?"

"Sure will."

She sat up and shed the nightgown. "Now let's get to serious things." And she kissed him, lying on her side facing him.

"Good. I am glad that is settled," he said and pulled the

covers up. Even with his own heater and her body, it felt like it might really be real cold overnight. Their coupling made it feel warmer.

Before dawn Slocum saddled her horse, and gave her the small derringer that Dan had given him. She knew how to use it.

"Just be careful," he said and clapped her on the butt before boosting her onto the horse.

In the saddle, she said, "They may send him reinforcements."

"I'll be ready."

She galloped off.

Having taken his prisoner out of the shed and led him up to the outside kitchen, Slocum fed him and then asked him more questions.

"How much did he pay you to kill her?"

"A hundred pesos."

"He know that I was here?"

"He knew someone came back with her."

"They got someone watching me now?"

The man shrugged.

Slocum tied him back up in a chair, then went to heat water and separate frijoles from sticks and rocks on the tabletop. He found some onions to chop up, fry, and add later. Then he chunked up some bacon, small fried it, and tossed it in with the beans. They'd have plenty to eat. If she didn't get back soon enough, he'd make some biscuits in her Dutch oven.

Mid-afternoon, the neighbor men started to arrive. Those who didn't know Slocum shook his hand and then acted grim about having heard Jena's story, but they'd come to help settle the matter.

"That's the worst thing I ever heard. What's Riddle

thinking, hiring this worthless pile of shit here to kill you and Jena?" one of the men said.

"He wants her ranch, and cheap," Slocum replied. "Jena needs this ranch to raise her kids. I hope you will all help her."

"We damn sure will," the man said. "She said you couldn't stay?"

"She's right, but I want this matter settled before I ride out."

"We can settle it in short order. The rest get here, we'll do like the Texas Rangers do and ride in on him in the early morning. Your beans sure smell good."

"Get a bowl. I made a big batch."

He didn't need to say more; the heavily armed outfit of older and younger men went to eating. Next he set into making sourdough biscuits and visiting with various men that came by and joined them.

Jena was back by mid-afternoon. She jumped off her horse, saying hi to everyone. One of the men took the horse and put it up for her. She stirred Slocum's beans with a paddle in the big pot and nodded her approval of his cooking venture. "You're doing great."

"You did good too," he said and made a wave at all the men already there.

She agreed with a little show of pride. "Lots more coming."

"These men would be enough, but the more there are, the better it will be."

"They told me we should ride up at dawn and confront him."

"Sounds all right to me."

There were twenty-five men and older boys eating his beans and biscuits for supper. Afterward they spread bedrolls on the ground. A few had a bottle or two they shared, but it was quiet after sundown. Slocum and Jena retired to the house, and in bed they snuggled and enjoyed themselves.

"You have spoiled me," she said and stretched slowly with her arms over her head, lying beside him.

"You'll get over it."

In the room's dim light, he saw her shake her head.

Then she said, "I borrowed enough flour and sugar from Jeb to make pancakes and syrup in the morning."

"We'll feed them all right. Wake me when you get up."

She agreed and crowded close to his back to hug him tight, and they slept. They rose in the night and made coffee and pancakes. Several of the men came over to help them. Others went to saddle their horses. By four A.M., they were ready to ride, with two hours to get to Riddle's ranch.

The posse rode in quiet with their prisoner, who had been silent despite the questions shot at him. Armed with rifles, they surrounded the house and Slocum said aloud, "Riddle, get out here. You resist, we'll shoot you down!"

"What the hell do you want?" He appeared half-dressed in the doorway.

"Who else is in there?" Slocum said.

"Jimmy, get out here. There's a hundred crazy people out here."

A tall, younger man came out without a shirt. Jena nodded at Slocum. "He's the one told me."

Slocum booted his horse up closer. "We have your man with us."

"'With us,' what the hell does that mean?" Riddle demanded.

"He said you shot Earl."

"How does he know? He wasn't there."

"But you and Jimmy were."

Riddle turned white over his words. "We . . . found . . . him dead. Apaches killed him." He looked at Jimmy. "Tell them.

"It wasn't my idea, I swear. He shot him, and he told me what I had to do."

A voice from the posse spoke out. "I say hang the whole damn lot of them."

That was word enough, and men rushed in to tie up both of them. "Get that Mexican! We're cleaning up this deal. Where we going to hang them?"

Slocum quieted them down. "We have witnesses," he said. "We can take them to the law. Let's vote."

Arms shot up. "Hang them!"

"Then do it right. Tie nooses and everyone here is sworn to secrecy. There will be questions."

"We need to bury their bodies and burn the nooses," one of the ranchers said.

"Good idea!" called another.

"I want to thank you for serving this cause," Slocum told them all. "I am taking Jena back to her ranch."

Men came and shook his hand, and then the two of them rode off. They were well away from the scene when they began to talk. He said, "There is never enough in vengeance to repair the damage done to you."

She agreed. "But now I can go get my children and start my life over."

"Yes, my friends may not want to let them go."

She laughed. "Before we go over there, will you spend a few days with me and we can check the ranch cattle?"

"I am in no rush."

"I am selfish."

"I understand. It has been trying."

They spent the next two days on a honeymoon and then went after the children. In Tombstone slocum bought an *Epitaph* to read the headline story.

AREA RANCHER IN A GRAVE?

Investigations continued when three fresh graves were discovered on a ranch in the Mule Shoe Mountain district. Sherman Riddle and Jimmy Nolan his ranch hand are all suspected to be buried up there, with a third person unknown. Sheriff John Behan calls it an ongoing investigation and says his men are questioning everyone. If you have any information on their disappearance, contact the sheriff's office.

"I guess they did it right." Slocum rolled up the paper and stuck it in his saddlebags.

"Where will you go next?" she asked.

"Oh, somewhere."

"Don't you ever get tired of moving around?"

"I am still alive."

"I know, but I'll be glad to be back to the ranch with my kids. I'll hire a couple of neighborhood boys to look after the cattle for me."

"You have any money?"

She shook her head. "I can borrow some till I sell some cattle."

He felt in his saddlebags and lifted out the heavy pouch of gold he'd taken off the prospector what seemed now so long ago. "Man that found this was killed by Apaches. He'd want you to have it. Enough in there to tide you over till you can make it."

She frowned and pulled the drawstring open. "This is all gold."

"No rocks either," he said, teasing her.

"How can I repay this?"

"No repayment. It is for you and the kids."

She began to cry.

He rode in close and hugged her shoulder. "Jena, the giver was killed by Apaches. He'd have wanted you and those kids to have a new start."

In late afternoon they reached the outskirts of the Mormon community. When they got in sight of the Morales farm, she said, "Oh no, that is Harry riding a pony."

He came out of the yard on his Shetland and waved at her. "Mom, Mom, look what they got me."

"I see it, Harry. I see it. I hope you are ready to go home?"

"I think so."

Alma was carrying Lena and came to meet them. Gordon got up from watching the boy ride the pony.

They had lots to talk about. Then the three females went inside, and Harry rode his pony around the yard.

"I got some information," Gordon began. "Two strangers were in St. David this week asking if you were around here."

"Thanks. I have one more mission. Will you be sure they get home all right?"

"I'll drive her wagon up there. She need anything?"

"No. She's fine. Her neighbor shot him, not the Apaches. But that's been handled. I'll see you again. You can tell her I had to leave."

"I understand."

He made the ride to her schoolhouse going across country. When he stopped and surveyed the country short of the whitewashed building, he hoped she had not left the school. There was no sign in the yucca-and-century-plant cover of anyone being around.

At the open door he dismounted, and hat off, he swept his hair back.

"Slocum, you're here," she said and came hurrying from the front of the empty classroom.

They kissed, and he herded her inside. His back against the wall inside, they kissed some more.

"There were two men here asking me about you a few days ago. I said you were down in Mexico."

He smiled down at her. "I heard about them. After this school session is over, you are going back to Kansas?"

"Yes, I think I can hold my head up there, and my father can use me."

"You will find a real man. You are too much woman not to find a real one."

She looked around, chewing on her lower lip. "I wish we had time and a place—"

"Thanks. You're a sweet woman. I am on my way out of here." Her faint perfume in his nose, he rocked her in his arms and savored her glorious body.

"God be with you, big man. I will pray for you."

They went outside, and he kissed her on the cheek. Then, before he stepped into the stirrup, from her pocket she took a new gray silk neckerchief and tied it around his neck. She waved good-bye as he rode off.

He rode long into the night. No woman to share his bed-roll that evening. He studied the North Star and Big Dipper. There were times when it became inconvenient for him to remain in the same spot. *Damn shame.*

Watch for

SLOCUM AND THE THREE FUGITIVES

418th novel in the exciting SLOCUM series
from Jove

Coming in December!

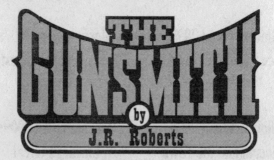